MATCHED, AUSTEN

A BEST FRIEND'S BROTHER ROMANCE

BRITNEY M. MILLS

CRYSTAL CANYON PUBLISHING

CHAPTER 1

Olivia Justice squeezed her mother's hand as she leaned over the metal railing on the hospital bed. Her mother slept soundly, her features calm and smooth. Moving her hand, Olivia pulled a section of hair away from her mother's eyes, tucking it back behind her ear. It was something her mother had done for her so many times over the years, usually when trying to get Olivia to wake up for school or work.

A knock came at the door, and Olivia was grateful for the distraction from the memories, from back when things in her life hadn't gotten so out of control.

Turning, Olivia took in a tall man in a white lab coat, clipboard in hand. Out of the corner of her eye, she saw her younger sister Scarlett scoot forward onto the front of her chair and grin like a fool. Now wasn't the time to flirt with someone.

"Hello, Dr. Turner." She batted her longer lashes several times. I had to turn away, having seen her flirtation routine one too many times and usually in the most inappropriate places.

"Miss Justice," he said with a curt nod.

It took some work to school her face, but Olivia couldn't have asked for a better way to shut down the vibes her sister was giving out than by using her surname.

The doctor turned and looked Olivia in the eyes. "Hello, I'm Dr. Turner. I've been going over your mother's case and tests for the past several weeks. Are you," he paused as he flipped the pages on the clipboard, "Olivia?"

"Yes. I've been, um, gone for a few weeks, but I'm back and not planning on going anywhere." The words tumbled out, and Olivia fought the lump swelling in her throat. She'd returned home the night before from the finale of *The Suitor*, a reality dating show set up by the matchmaking company, Love, Austen, and had barely made it to her bed before falling asleep. Several weeks on an emotional rollercoaster had taken its toll, and she still felt the exhaustion weighing down on her.

Scarlett sat up straighter than Olivia had ever seen. "My sister was looking for love on a dating show. She didn't win, unfortunately," she said, forcing a frown.

Why did the doctor need to know all this? If anything, it just made her look bad, like she was putting her dating life above the wellness of her mother.

The man smiled with recognition, and Olivia was sure he winked at Scarlett. What was going on between them? So much for her sister getting shut down.

"Do you have information on my mother's condition?" Olivia tried to make her voice sound even, but there was still a hint of accusation. If Scarlett was going after their mother's doctor, she needed to learn some boundaries, like not bantering with him when decisions needed to be made about their mother's care.

Nodding, Dr. Turner said, "Yes, I do. After several tests

this past week and from observation, we believe your mother is showing signs of moderate dementia."

Olivia's mind whirred, pulling up all the information she could remember about what she'd heard and learned since her mother had been diagnosed with Alzheimer's four years ago.

"Moderate dementia? Already?" She turned and looked at her mother. The face of Peggy Justice was serene, without pain or worry… for the moment.

"Her sleep patterns have changed to where she's sleeping more during the day, and she's drawn into herself more than before. When she does speak, everything is muddled and confused."

Words Olivia had hoped to avoid hearing for several more years. She scooted to the edge of the chair, as if that would propel her to find a way to stop the decline of her mother's health so soon. "What do we need to do?"

"We've started several more tests and observations, but results won't be in for a few days. We'll keep you updated on our findings." The man licked his lips and stared right at Olivia. There was no joking in his eyes, meaning Olivia needed to internalize all of it, knowing that instead of finding a cure, she needed to enjoy the time she had left with her mother.

Nodding, she said, "Thank you, doctor. Please do contact us the moment you find out anything. My number is there in the chart."

He gave her a curt nod and turned to Scarlett, winking again. Scarlett waved and pursed her lips out, making her look like a duck. Once the man had left the room, Olivia turned to her, anger flaring in her chest.

"Okay, spill. What's going on there?" She pointed her thumb toward the door and raised her eyebrows.

Scarlett inspected her nails, avoiding Olivia's gaze. "I don't know what you're talking about."

"How often does a doctor wink at his patient's daughter?" She narrowed her eyes, waiting for a response.

Letting out a giggle, Scarlett said, "We've been dating for the last few weeks."

"Dating? Mom's doctor?"

"Yeah, so what? It's nice to know that such a kind, generous man is taking care of our mother." Scarlett looked toward the door and smiled, sighing.

Rolling her eyes, Olivia said, "You mean taking care of you."

With a scowl, Scarlett said, "Oh, please. Like you haven't been doing the same thing? At least I visited Mom during that time."

Olivia dropped her mother's hand and stood, trying to breathe in and out as much as possible before exploding.

"Don't try to tell me why I did or didn't come here." It came out in a harsh whisper, more than she could muster if the tears were allowed to flow. "With Mom's care and our living expenses, we can't live like this forever. We'll run out of money sooner rather than later, and I was trying to do something to help that."

"By dating a professional hockey player? Well, that went over well." Scarlett folded her arms over her chest, glaring at Olivia.

Raising her hands, Olivia bit her tongue for a moment. "I didn't know that before we stepped on set. I came out of it with a new friend and some money to go toward the bills."

The past six weeks had been a whirlwind, and Olivia still couldn't believe she'd been on a reality dating show. She'd been asked to participate by Meg Austen, the owner of Love, Austen. It had taken some thought but since some of her profile matched up with Carson Carver, one of the stars of the Boston Breeze, she figured it couldn't hurt to try. She didn't like to think she'd done it for the money but coming in third place had helped pay off some of the ever accumulating bills.

In the end, she'd gotten close with the woman who was meant for Carson, Ruby Hunter. Seeing the two of them together in a second chance at love made her wish for a first chance with someone special. A certain brown-haired, brown-eyed someone popped into her mind, and she shook her head, knowing that wouldn't happen, not while she was still trying to figure out her current life.

Softening, Scarlett walked over, holding her arms out. She wrapped Olivia in a hug, pulling her back to the present. "I know, I'm sorry. It just seemed more glamorous than staying home, you know."

Olivia nodded against her sister's shoulder and said, "I know. But I promise it wasn't all that you imagine. There was a lot of drama, and a lot is staged for audience ratings." Pulling away from her sister, she said, "We need to look for jobs. The life insurance will only last so long now that the medical expenses are going up."

Scarlett bit her lip. "I was afraid you would say that. What about the salon? They won't take you back?"

"No," Olivia shook her head, sitting in the chair again. "Cynthia told me she wouldn't hold my job if I left for that long."

"There's got to be other salons looking for a stylist."

Olivia frowned. "I haven't had the chance to find one yet. That's what today will be for. Care to join me?"

"Let me have one more day of bliss. I'll start on the job search tomorrow." Scarlett sat back down, smiling at something on her phone.

Leaning over, Olivia kissed her mother's forehead, wishing she'd open her eyes and beam at her like she used to.

Moderate dementia. It only meant their time together was growing short, and Olivia was lost as to how she could help. Since her father's death, she'd been the one to make sure bills were paid, and they didn't go crazy when it came to spending. The financial knowledge her father had taught her throughout the years had only helped to make their lives a bit easier as her sister thought money just magically appeared from a credit card.

"What are you off to do now?" she asked Scarlett.

"Greg, uh, Dr. Turner gets off in a half hour, so I'll hang out here until he's done."

Blowing out a breath, she asked, "Is it getting serious between you two?"

Scarlett nodded, her smile lighting up her face. "We've talked about the future several times."

Reaching out her hand, Olivia grabbed her sister's and looked her in the eyes. "Just be careful."

"I will be." The two of them embraced before Olivia turned and walked out the door, leaving Scarlett in the room, stuck to her phone.

Olivia wished she could have a few more hours to relax at home, but she knew she needed to find a job if she wanted to keep her mother in The Jones Alzheimer Institute. She just hoped she'd find a place hiring and soon.

CHAPTER 2

Dawson Holt picked up a stack of papers and straightened them, giving them a final pound on the desk. The sun had disappeared behind the horizon, the last few rays of sunlight lighting up the darkening sky. It had been a longer day than he was used to, starting with several conference calls at five thirty that morning and then the regular production and management meetings throughout the rest of the day.

He saw the blinking red light on his phone and heard the voice of his secretary. Leaning forward, he said, "What's up, Barbara? What are you still doing here?"

The older woman made a funny noise and then said, "Someone's got to make you look good for that big meeting tomorrow, and it sure won't be Angela, even though she tries to sweet talk you at every turn." Dawson sat back and chuckled, trying not to interrupt the woman while on a rampage.

"I'm not that dense, Barb."

"I was hoping you weren't, but I have to check." The woman went silent for a moment and then said, "Oh! Sorry. I buzzed you because Adelyn called and insisted she talk to you. I told her you were on an important call, and she hung up."

Dawson sobered. "Okay, thanks." A bitter taste rose in his throat, and he swallowed, hoping to get rid of it. But instead of clearing completely, it lingered. It could have been a metaphor for his dating life, but he chose to push that thought aside.

"When are you going to cut that girl loose?"

Rubbing his hands over his face, Dawson leaned his elbows on the desk, holding his forehead. "I've been meaning to. I just haven't gotten around to it.

"You don't still want to marry her, do you? It's been a month since you proposed. Not that my opinion matters all that much, but I'd be jumping at the chance to marry you, if I were twenty years younger and not married to the love of my life already."

Dawson grinned at that. Was it weird he was having a personal conversation over the phone with his secretary who sat just feet outside his door? More like a lecture than a conversation. He picked up his suit coat and briefcase, shutting down his computer.

Walking out to the woman's desk, he said, "I'll figure it out, Barb. Thanks for all you do. Head out. We'll get everything polished in the morning."

She gave him a hesitant look before pulling her purse out of the bottom drawer and walking out with him. Once she made it to the T-station on the corner, he turned back to the parking garage and walked up to the fourth level, where his car was parked.

Getting in, he stuck the key into the ignition and turned. He usually took the train home as well, but he'd been late for a meeting that morning and had driven in.

Right as he put his hand on the shifter, his phone rang. He turned the screen to see it said Adelyn Garrett.

She's not going to leave me alone.

His relationship with Adelyn Garrett had been a tumultuous one. They'd been dating for the past two years and so far, Dawson felt like he'd gotten about as far as a hamster running in a wheel. He'd proposed, in the hopes that it would break the cycle, and in a way it had. Since she'd told him she didn't know if she wanted to marry him, his heart had begun to distance itself from her.

Maybe it was the comfort of the known that kept him from officially breaking up with her, but he hadn't told her they were done yet. Reflecting on Barbara's words, he swiped the screen, holding the phone to his ear.

"Hello?"

"It's good to hear you're still alive, Dawson." Adelyn giggled a little too loud, meaning she wanted something. "I was beginning to worry that you're screening my calls."

"Long day." The sound of his voice matched the exhaustion in his body.

"Not too long, I hope," she said, trying to make her voice teasing. "Come dancing with me tonight."

Dawson shook his head harder than he'd meant to, but it felt good. Now he just needed to put that into words and convince her. He was ready for the next step, to settle down and begin a family. But it seemed all she cared about was keeping things the same, going out every night and enjoying life in the city.

"Not tonight. It's Tuesday, and I've got another long day tomorrow. Maybe some other time."

Silence answered him on the other end, and he had to pull the phone away to see if the call was still connected. They'd known each other for a few years, but it seemed time had changed them, something he'd come to realize more and more in the past couple of weeks.

"I'm still thinking about it, you know. Your question,"

Adelyn said, her voice light, usually meaning she was trying to appease him.

Irritation flared to life in Dawson's stomach, and he gripped the steering wheel until his knuckles turned white.

"I'm beginning to think you aren't as serious about us as I was." He pressed the accelerator, taking advantage of a hole in the traffic.

"Was? Dawson, don't give up on me yet. We've had some great times. You know how my parents' marriage fizzled out at the end. I'm just making sure to weigh the options. You know I care about you, right?" Adelyn's voice started out pleading but by the end, it had risen at least an octave, and she sounded as though she would get down on her knees and beg.

Did he know she cared about him? That didn't translate to love.

"Weigh the options? Adelyn, maybe we just need a break." The words were out of his mouth before he'd fully thought it through. But they were out, and he held his breath, curious what she would say.

"A break?" The ice in her tone sent a chill down his back, but the more he thought about it, the more he liked the idea. They'd been together for so long, maybe time away would be a good thing. Help them both think through what they wanted.

He blew out a breath. "I just think we've got a lot going on with our schedules, and we could use a little time away."

A month ago, all he could think about was the wedding they'd have and the future family they'd raise together. Sure, his parents' marriage hadn't been all roses, but they'd worked together to raise him and his brother and sister. He thought he'd just have to shoulder through it, make it work. But that wouldn't help if she didn't put in some effort as well.

"I don't think—"

"I've got to head home. Have a good night." He ended the call before she had a chance to respond, not in the mood to hear another lame excuse. For some reason, the idea of them being on a break relieved him of a weight on his chest. Barbara had a point. Maybe he needed to move on and find someone else.

CHAPTER 3

The job search the day before had been a big waste of time. After scouring the classifieds on several websites, Olivia had contacted them all and even walked into other salons, asking for any openings. Time and time again, the managers or owners shook their heads, making Olivia feel a little like a beggar.

Now, checking her email, she had a long list of unopened ones and as she clicked through each one, she read a different form of, "Sorry, we don't have any openings," or "The position has been filled."

Scarlett trudged down the stairs, looking as though she'd slept in the clothes she'd worn last night. Olivia pasted on a smile, hoping to fake happiness until she felt it.

"How did last night go?" she asked, as Scarlett took a seat next to her on the couch.

Scarlett curled up on the edge of the couch, tucking one of the throw pillows to her chest and closing her eyes. "It was a lot of fun. Greg is so sweet, and he's the life of the party. Right now I have a pounding headache though."

With a chuckle, Olivia said, "That's what you get for coming in at three in the morning."

Sitting up long enough to open her eyes a slit, Scarlett said, "You heard me?"

"A herd of elephants would have made less noise."

Scarlett shrugged and fell back onto the armrest, her breathing evening out.

Olivia made sure to angle the laptop away from her sister as she checked the bank account. It took only a few seconds to calculate just how long her small family could survive on its contents. And that was without any special tests or treatments for her mother. They'd been able to survive this long with the life insurance from her father's passing and the small earnings she'd gotten from working as a beautician. But that wouldn't be the case for too long if she didn't replace her income.

Reflecting over her time on *The Suitor*, a wave of sadness filled her. She'd had such hope that things would work out, that because she was one of the matches, she'd win the heart of the guy and be taken care of. It had turned into another one of her fantasies, where she would be rescued from her new life to one that matched her childhood. A foolish dream on the flip side. But if there was one thing the show had taught her, it was that she would find a way for things to work out.

The money she'd been awarded from the show had been deposited that morning and while it sounded like a lot of money when they announced it, after taxes and fees, it was much slimmer than she would have liked.

Moving to the small table in the kitchen nook, Olivia pulled out her phone, sipping from a mug of hot chocolate. She browsed several websites, hoping some neon sign would point to the best job the world could offer a twenty-seven-year-old college dropout.

The doorbell rang. Scarlett hadn't so much as stirred, her eyes closed and her breathing heavy, so Olivia stood and opened the door.

"Ella! What are you doing here?" Olivia looked around the entry, mentally trying to remember if everything was clean and put away. Her best friend hadn't judged the Justice family when they'd had to downsize from the large home in Newton to the small basement apartment in Brighton. She was just about the only one from what felt like a previous life to ever come over.

"I was in the neighborhood and thought I'd stop by." Her light-brown hair looked almost perfect at eight in the morning. Olivia absentmindedly felt the messy bun on the top of her head, hoping it didn't make her look like Medusa with all the stray curls.

With a frown, Olivia said, "Please, what would bring you to this part of town so early in the morning?"

"You, of course. I haven't seen you since you went gallivanting off to be on a reality dating show, and I missed my best friend." Ella stuck out her lower lip, and Olivia laughed. "Looks like your sister had a rough night."

Ushering her into the kitchen, Olivia motioned to the chair next to the table, and Ella sat.

"Yeah, that much didn't change in the last six weeks. Orange juice?" Olivia called from next to the fridge.

"Yes, please."

Olivia poured from the pitcher on the counter and set the glass down in front of Ella, resuming her seat to the left.

"How can you drink hot chocolate when it's so hot outside? It's over eighty-seven degrees and not even ten in the morning."

Olivia took a sip and grinned. "There's no time limit for hot chocolate. And we live in the basement, so it's always so cool in the morning."

"You're crazy," Ella said, sipping her juice.

"And I can't believe you said I 'gallivanted' off. If it's anyone's fault I've been gone for so long, it's yours, girl." Olivia pointed a finger at Ella, who swatted the hand away. Ella had given Olivia a gift certificate for Love, Austen on her last birthday, which led to the experience with *The Suitor*.

"Maybe a little bit, but can't a girl help her best friend find love? I only gave you a matchmaking package. You were the one who agreed to go on the show."

Scrunching her nose, Olivia sighed. "True. It was a roller-coaster, that's for sure."

Ella stuck out her hand and grabbed Olivia's forearm. "I still can't believe you did it. How was it, really? I watched the highlights video, but what was it like behind the scenes?"

"Just like you can imagine it would be with twelve women vying for one guy. Dramatic!" The two girls chuckled a bit at that. "I got to know the girl who won. Ruby is such a sweet girl, and she's over the moon that she and Carson are back together."

"What about you? Any guys I need to know about?" Olivia felt a poke in her ribs, and she wiggled away so Ella couldn't do it again.

"Haha. Funny. I've been back from the Berkshires a whole two days. If it hasn't happened before now, I doubt it would happen that fast." Olivia closed her eyes and yawned.

"Why do you laugh? You're gorgeous, funny, and hard working. You're like the perfect combo." Ella lifted the orange juice to her lips, taking a long pull before setting it back on the table.

Pulling at a piece of hair that had fallen out of the bun, Olivia twisted it around her finger and said, "Really? Most guys like the straight-haired chicks, not girls who have an afro on especially humid days."

"Oh, please! Remember in seventh grade when I got a perm so I could be just like you?'

"And you washed it out that night because you couldn't stand the smell. Yes, I remember that." Olivia grinned. "Those awkward years were the worst."

"Your hair looks amazing now, by the way. Maybe it's all the expertise of styling."

Olivia scoffed. "Expertise doesn't pay the bills though. I just need to relax and know that I'll find a job. It *will* happen."

"Exactly. Positivity is the key." They were silent for a moment before a startled look crossed Ella's face.

Wagging her pointer finger, Olivia shook her head. "No, no. I know that look, and it usually doesn't mean good things."

Ella frowned. "What do you mean? I have a great opportunity for you. At least I think it is."

Olivia rolled her eyes and leaned forward, crossing her arms on the table. "Am I going to regret saying I'm a little curious?"

With a light smack, Ella grinned. "Of course not. I was talking to the Bourdens yesterday, and they're looking for a nanny for the summer."

"The Bourdens, as in the people who bought my parents' summer home?"

"Yep, the very same." Ella looked a bit more hesitant now, and Olivia folded her arms, trying to process what should have been one simple piece of information.

"It's July. Shouldn't Tonya have started looking sooner?" Olivia bit her tongue, knowing she didn't need to spill every thought in her mind, even if it was to Ella.

The Bourdens had bought the Nantucket house Olivia's family used to own soon after David Justice died. As relieving as it was to not have the burden of the place anymore with all its upkeep, she still ached as she thought about all the memories from every summer since she could remember. She and Ella had become best friends there, and it held some of her fondest memories.

"Their nanny ran off to get married to some guy after working for three weeks, and she's been struggling to find a new one."

Olivia laughed. "That sounds like something I want to do." She paused, rolling her eyes to emphasize the sarcasm. "If the one nanny can't hack it, what makes you think I will?"

"Because you're amazing with kids. And Tonya told me they're willing to triple the pay if you can start right away."

"Wait, you already discussed this with her before talking to me about it?" Olivia ground her teeth together, not a fan of being played.

Ella shook her head. "No, not you specifically. She just asked if I knew of anyone willing and available to do the job." She raised her eyebrows and opened her eyes as wide as they would go, which was her way of showing she was telling the truth. "It would be perfect, Liv. Just like old times."

"Our summers weren't spent tending bratty children." Olivia blew on her hot chocolate before taking a small sip.

"Oh, come on. They aren't that bad," Ella said, giving Olivia's arm a gentle push. "They're actually really good kids. Besides, we can hang out all summer, and you can help me finalize the details for the wedding. I only have two months until I move to Europe for an undetermined amount of time." Ella's eyes opened wide, and Olivia knew the pleading look was about to make an appearance.

"Give me her number. If I don't hear back from any of these salons, I'll call her." With the money she'd gotten from the show, they would be okay for a few more weeks, but Olivia didn't want to chance going too long without income coming in. She knew she couldn't count on Scarlett for help, and their mother's bills were piling up with all the tests and procedures. That was never a worry though. As long as the doctors took care of her mother, Olivia would do what she could to pay for it.

After spending a few more minutes chatting, Ella left, pleading with Olivia to call about the job. Just what she needed. At twenty-seven, she should be on her way to having her own kids, not nannying for someone else.

CHAPTER 4

$\mathcal{D}$awson's mind turned through the things he'd need to accomplish in the next few months. The family company had several contracts he was trying to tie up, which would nearly double the amount of production needed, creating more jobs. One thing he loved about being CEO of Holt Packaging was that he could make it possible for more people to support their families. The downside of that was when clients turned to a competitor or went out of business, the ripple affect extended much longer than he'd thought before taking over the company.

He focused on Angela's monotone voice coming from the other end of the table, explaining the numbers from the last month. It was a longer staff meeting than he had the patience for, and he would have loved to get up and leave. Yet, as the boss, there were certain things he had to suffer through.

Once Angela finished her presentation and sat, Dawson looked to his left and said, "Jeffrey, where are we with the new materials? Have we received the shipment of samples from the manufacturer in Chicago?"

"We have. Production is looking it over in the next few days and will let us know—"

The door opened, causing everyone in the room to turn. Dawson's stomach dropped as he saw Adelyn standing in the door.

With a wide grin on her face, she waved and said, "Hello, everyone!" Barbara came into view a few seconds later, looking out of breath. She made a stabbing motion in Adelyn's direction, and Dawson had to cover his mouth to keep from laughing. She'd never been a fan of the woman, and he understood why.

He stood, took a few steps in her direction, and whispered, "What do you need, Adelyn? We're in the middle of a staff meeting, and we need to get back to it." His snappy tone did nothing to curb her smile.

"Can I talk to you for a moment?" she asked, pointing to the door.

Pinching the bridge of his nose, he nodded. He turned to face the table and said, "Okay, Jeffrey, keep the meeting going. Update me when I get back."

He walked out and pulled the door closed, taking a split second to compose himself. Spinning on his heel, he looked down at her, keeping his expression as stone faced as possible. "What do you need that's important enough to interrupt my morning meeting?"

Adelyn reached forward and put her hand into his. "I just feel like you're really distant lately. I barely see you anymore, and I wanted to do something with you tonight."

"Again, it's been a long week, and today is Thursday, meaning I still have to work tomorrow. I'm not in the mood to be out super late. Besides, we're on a break."

She twisted her hand until her fingers were intertwined with his, her eyes boring into his. "I didn't agree to a break."

Her lips twitched, her expression softening. "We could just go to dinner or something. And talk."

Dawson looked to the wall for a second before turning his gaze back to Adelyn. As much as he wanted to be angry at her, sometimes it was easier to comply the first time and get it over with. When Adelyn decided on something, she kept at it until it worked out in her favor. But the fact that she hadn't been like that about marrying him still cut deep. He wanted to know what it was that kept her from saying yes right then, or any other moments before that.

One dinner. That's all this would be. And maybe he'd know what to change for any future relationships.

"Fine. You pick the place."

* * *

Adelyn had requested Top Shelf, and being a friend of the owner, Carson Carver, Dawson had been able to get a table. She'd been running late from an afternoon meeting at work and asked him to meet her there.

Sitting in the back, Dawson played with the fork and knife, trying to keep himself occupied. After a few more minutes, he pulled out his phone and checked emails.

"I'm sorry I'm late. I feel like all I've done today is sit in traffic." Adelyn took her purse off and slung it across the back of the chair, not moving in for a kiss like she used to. She opened the menu and looked it over. "Is Carson here today?"

"No, he's with Ruby." Dawson picked up the goblet filled with water and took a sip.

"Who's Ruby?" She pursed her lips and scrunched her nose as she focused on him again.

Taking in a deep breath, Dawson let it out slowly. He'd only told her a dozen times that Carson had become something like *The Bachelor* and was now with his high school sweetheart once again. He'd had only seen the last two episodes of *The Suitor*, wanting to support his friend but not wanting to get into all the drama that these shows usually entailed.

When he thought of that last episode, he'd been surprised to see one of his sister's friends, Olivia Justice. She looked beautiful in the evening gown, with her hair and makeup done. Growing up next door during the summers on Nantucket, she'd always been a natural beauty and a smart girl. Something about those simpler times caused an ache in his chest.

What still bugged him was why she was on a dating show in the first place. He knew all too well how time changed people, but Liv's sweet demeanor and kindness seemed like it would clash with a show like that.

Shaking his head a bit, he focused on Adelyn. Although he shouldn't have done it, his mind compared Adelyn with Liv. From the way Adelyn always talked about celebrities and the latest reality show, she might have been a better match for the show. He'd have to ask Carson more about the experience. He was curious about Liv and what she'd been up to the past few years.

"Hello? Dawson? Are you alive in there?"

A waiter came in, and Dawson mentally kicked himself for thinking about someone from his past in comparison to the girl he'd been dating for a couple of years. They ordered and after he left, Dawson turned to Adelyn.

"How did your marketing meeting go today? Are you taking your father's company to new heights?" Apparently, he wasn't ready to talk about their relationship.

Adelyn unrolled the cloth napkin around the silverware and smoothed it onto her lap. "Going well. I started a few new ad campaigns on social media, so I'll see where the results are in the next few days." She took a sip of water and then said, "You should let me look at your marketing plan. I'm sure I could give you some pointers on how to increase revenue and sales."

Through clenched teeth, he said, "Ella does that for us, but thank you." This wasn't the first time she'd offered to do the marketing for his company, but he still felt like Ella's experience had strengthened the company over the last three years. He didn't want to mess with a good thing.

Flipping her hair to the side, she gave him a side eye. "Well, if she needs some time off while she plans her wedding, just let me know. Anything to help you out, Dawson bunny."

Watching her, he tried to sort through his emotions. She was beautiful and a bit more controlling than he liked at times, but maybe he needed that in his life. Things hadn't worked out with many other women as his schedule was demanding, but she'd stuck with him throughout the past two years. Surely that earned her points for loyalty.

He ran a hand through his hair, trying to keep up with the fast pace of her words, babbling on about her marketing strategy for Garrett Cakes.

He ate slowly, only making a few comments here and there when she asked a question. It wasn't something he should decide so quickly. Over the last week, he'd made a list of all the pros and cons of their relationship, trying to decide what he wanted. That method had served him well throughout the past few years as head of a packaging busi-ness. But for some reason, it was different when it wasn't a business decision.

"Are you feeling all right?" Adelyn asked, pulling him out of his latest thoughts.

"Yeah, I'm good. Just looking forward to an early night. I'm beat."

"You should rest up then. Maybe by next week you can come out to events and things with me again." She cut into her piece of chicken, placing the small bite into her mouth and chewing thoughtfully.

Dawson pasted on a smile and said, "We'll see."

Rest. That kind of relaxation would have to be somewhere outside the city. A visual of the family's summer home on Nantucket popped into his mind, and he had the urge to go. But with work as crazy as it had been, would he be able to escape for a few days?

He could take his laptop with him and work in the mornings, allowing him some time to enjoy the fresh sea breeze and hang out where it was more relaxed. And Ella would be there until her wedding. Looking up at Adelyn, he said, "I think a break is a good idea. I'll head to Nantucket for the weekend and see if I can figure out how to slow down a bit."

"Oh, I wish I could come with you, but there's so much going on right now. Raincheck?" She didn't so much as glance up at him. When had things changed so much? Or had they been like this for a long time? A pang of sadness and regret hit him in the chest at that thought.

"Adelyn, I meant what I said earlier." He swallowed, glancing at the bright white tablecloth as he called up the courage to finish his thoughts. "I think an overall break would be good. Give us a couple of weeks and see where we're at?"

Adelyn reached her hand forward and covered Dawson's fist sitting on the table. "You'll still call me, right?"

Dawson tossed his head back and chuckled. "No, because we're on a break. We should both take a step back and refocus, see what it is we really want."

Her face first showed him the shock and sadness of his words, but then there was a gleam in her eye, and she seemed more willing.

"A break. That might just be the thing I need." She tapped her lips with her pointer finger and nodded. "Okay."

That went a lot easier than he'd expected. Now what was the catch?

Paying the bill, Dawson sat back a moment, thinking about a weekend on Nantucket. A surge of excitement flowed through him, and he couldn't wait to pack and head out. He'd leave on the first ferry over the next morning and maybe have some summer fun like he used to.

CHAPTER 5

"I can't believe we're going to spend another summer on Nantucket together. It's been forever!" Ella's voice rose higher with every word, and Olivia had to pull the phone away.

"I hope it will be fun. It's definitely not where I saw my life going right now." Olivia pressed a stack of shirts into her large suitcase and then sank down onto the bed. Five days of searching for a job as a cosmetologist yielded nothing, and she'd finally broken down and called Mrs. Bourden. She was set to start at the beginning of the week.

"You'll be great as a nanny. Besides, that's one of the best jobs because you can do whatever you want while you entertain the kids."

Says the youngest child who never babysat in her life.

Although Olivia and Ella had grown up with a privileged life in most respects, Olivia's mother had made sure she'd been given plenty of chores around the house, as well as babysitting jobs for the people in the neighborhood. She'd always called it a good lesson in mothering, and Olivia still wondered if it was worth the trouble. The thought of those little nuggets of wisdom coming to an end because of her mother's health caused an ache to form in her chest.

"When are you coming out here then?" Ella's voice called her back from her sorrow.

"Um, I just finished laundry, so I'm packing right now. I don't start until Monday, so probably Saturday night?"

"Don't be silly. Get packed up and come stay with me for the weekend. It will be just like old times."

Those 'old times' made Olivia more nostalgic than she'd been since they'd sold the summer home. She just hoped she could survive the summer with the Bourden twins. At five, the boy and girl sounded like typical active kids, and Olivia knew she'd have to come up with activity after activity to keep them busy and out of trouble. But it was a paying position, and she couldn't turn down triple the wage.

"Hello? Earth to Liv."

"Sorry. That might be nice. I need to see my mom before I head out, so I'll call you when I'm on my way."

Hanging up, she threw another stack of shirts into her suitcase. She was both excited and nervous to head back to one of the most magical places she hadn't visited in several years. Pulling a few pairs of shoes from her closet, she just hoped it lived up to her expectations.

* * *

PACKING TOOK LESS THAN AN HOUR, and Olivia finished before lunch. She bought a sandwich from the corner market and walked to the bus stop, dragging her luggage along with her. Guilt wrapped itself around her chest as she thought of leaving her mother again for the next two months. Sure, she'd left her for the show, but that was before her mother's condition had worsened. How much time would she have left to visit, hoping Peggy Justice would recognize her oldest daughter? Then again, if she couldn't remember Olivia, it was almost like losing her every time she walked into the care center.

Not feeling like being crowded with several people on the bus, she held out her hand as a taxi approached. It was a splurge but at least she wouldn't be lugging her bags on and off at each transfer.

"Where are you heading, ma'am?" the driver asked.

"The Jones Alzheimer Institute."

After the man had loaded her luggage, she slipped inside, relishing for the coolness of the seats compared to the humidity outside. The ride didn't take long, and she paid the driver after he unloaded her suitcases.

Wheeling the bags into the building, she walked straight to her mother's room, leaving the suitcases next to the wall just inside the door. She heard the beeps of the machines and saw a form lying on the bed, the face blocked from her view by the railing.

"Hey, Mom. I wanted to say hey before I head out for work." Taking a seat next to the bed, Olivia was surprised to see her mother's head turn and her eyes focus on her.

"Livvy? What are you doing?" Her voice sounded an octave higher than Olivia was used to, but the fact that her mother was awake and recognized her made her heart leap in her chest.

Reaching forward, Olivia grasped her mother's hand and squeezed, grateful she'd decided to stop there first. "I've got a job on Nantucket for the summer, Mom. I'll come back and see you as often as I can though." Gulping around the lump in her throat, she continued, "Scarlett is staying at the house and will make sure to keep me updated on everything."

"Nantucket? You love going there. Are you bringing your dollies this time?" Her mother's smile struck a chord in Olivia's chest. The childhood nickname and mention of dolls must have been from memories over twenty years ago and the excitement Olivia had felt at being recognized shrunk.

"No, Mom. I'm going to be a nanny for the Bourden family. They bought our home there. But I'll be able to hang out with Ella. She's getting married in a few months."

Her mother leaned forward, as if ready to divulge some conspiracy. Her eyes looked clearer at this angle, and a mischievous grin took over her expression. "Make sure to get another kiss from Dawson. He's a good boy." She reached up and patted Olivia's cheek softly.

Olivia's thoughts swirled, and her cheeks burned. "How do you know about that?" Was her mom's mind in the distant past or closer?

"A mother always knows these things. You looked like you were floating on a cloud for the whole ride home after last time we left Nantucket."

Olivia felt her cheeks burn, still not sure how her mother could've known about her kissing Ella's older brother. Sure, she'd had a thing for him since the sixth grade, but she'd never told anyone about that night in Nantucket over four years ago. The night when Dawson took her to the lighthouse and gave her first real kiss.

Thinking back on it now, Olivia still got butterflies flying up in her stomach. She'd been kissed and had kissed boys throughout high school and beauty school, but there was something about the way Dawson's lips met hers that'd seemed to electrify everything. It had been the one memory she went back to from that summer, the pinnacle of her happy life. The days after, it seemed like the world was sliding out from under her.

She could picture his face even now, his dark-brown hair accentuating the light-brown irises and strong jaw. Just as quickly as the emotions had begun, Olivia shut them down, knowing her chance with him was just a fairytale. Their kiss was just a part of the moment, after a summer of being with each other every day.

There had never been an understanding between them, never a define-the-relationship talk, and Olivia had chalked it up to a sweet summer kiss, even though it was more of a summer friendship. Her father had passed weeks later, and her world had gone into upheaval with all the changes.

She'd seen in one of the society papers that he was dating the daughter of the Cake King, Garrett Cakes. Olivia had never loved the spotlight and was thankful her parents had kept her and Scarlett out of it as much as possible. Olivia was nothing more than an outcast in upper society now, something that hurt more than she wanted to admit.

"How are you feeling, Mom?" Olivia locked eyes with her mother's but the clarity that had been there moments before was gone. Her mother sank back, yanking her hand from Olivia's and burying herself beneath the blankets.

Trying not to let the tears fall, Olivia stood and moved to the door. "It was good to see you. I'll come back in a week or two to check up on you." Then in a softer tone, she said, "I miss you, Mom."

She turned and pulled her luggage out the door just as the first tears fell, not stopping to wipe them away. Why did everything have to change so drastically? Her childhood had been magical, and her teen years a dream. But at the rate life was going now, Olivia was ready to say goodbye to her twenties, wishing there were some cure for all the hurt and pain she'd been through in that time.

Hailing another cab outside the building, Olivia gave instructions to take her to the Hyannis ferry. She was glad she was heading out now, knowing how hard it would be to go back to her home after the past few minutes. She needed Ella's never-ending happiness to help her get through the next few weeks. But stepping foot on Nantucket would dig up some of its own emotions, and she hoped she'd be able to get through it.

CHAPTER 6

It was already later than he wanted to leave the office on Friday, but Dawson dropped his car off at home and took a cab to the ferry. Even though he'd planned to only stay the weekend, he felt more comfortable having the car at home rather than in the parking lot for days.

When the car stopped, he was still on his phone, checking some of the details from the meeting he'd had to attend that morning. He had to agree with Barbara that many of the employees working for the company knew what they were doing. Given the opportunity to work on their actual jobs was already paying off, as evidenced by the information in the emails. It made him breathe easier, knowing that a few days off wouldn't completely derail the company.

With luggage in hand, he strode over and waited in line at the ticket booth. He moved up a couple of times before putting his phone away and looking at the scenery around him.

In line right in front of him, he saw a girl a few inches shorter than his six-foot-one-inch frame, her blond hair flying around her face with a gust of wind. She turned her head as she tried to pull at a strand of hair stuck in her mouth, and Dawson recognized her.

"Liv? Liv Justice?"

She turned, her eyes going wide with horror before she gave him a hesitant smile. "Dawson. How are you?"

A sea of memories swam through his mind at the sound of her voice, and he couldn't help but grin.

"I'm good. You look great. I haven't seen you since…"

She waved him off and looked down at the sidewalk. "After the funeral."

Dawson felt bad for bringing it up, knowing how hard it'd been for her to get through the loss of her father. "You're heading to Nantucket?" He pointed to the ticket booth as they took another step forward, one passenger still in front of Olivia.

She sighed, tucking a piece of hair behind her ear. "Yeah. The Bourdens needed a nanny. Since I need a job, I figured why not?" A slight bitterness tinged her words.

It was her turn next at the ticket booth, but Dawson walked up next to her, leaning over to speak to the woman behind the glass. "Two please."

Liv turned to look at him. "You don't have to do that."

Pushing his credit card through the small opening, he grinned. "Yes, I do. It's a momentous occasion. Liv Justice returning to Nantucket after a long sabbatical." His voice went a little louder with each word, and she looked like she was ready to cover his mouth with her hand to get him to shut up. Lowering his voice, he gave her a small smile. "The least I can do is buy your ferry ticket. Maybe I can convince you to sit by me, so we can catch up on the way over."

Her cheeks turned rosy, and Dawson's face relaxed, an odd excitement filling him. Seeing her in person brought back a flood of memories, and he felt like a schoolboy, trying to talk to a girl but stumbling over every word.

The woman behind the booth slid two tickets and Dawson's credit card through the small opening and turned to look behind them, beckoning forward the next person in line.

Dawson and Liv walked to the ferry, taking a seat near the front bow. He turned to her, trying to decide which of the questions pounding around in his mind would be the best to start with.

"Tell me what you've been up to in the past four years. Nantucket in the summer has never been the same since you've been gone." He gave her a half-smile, and she looked skeptical.

"I'm sure life has just stopped in its tracks since I left." He caught onto her sarcasm and laughed.

"Well, you did leave a large void needing to be filled."

She cocked her head to the side and half-closed one eye. Folding her arms against her chest, she asked, "What did you use to fill it then?"

Dawson frowned. He'd forgotten that her quick wit would require a more fleshed-out story. She'd always been able to read beneath the surface of normal conversation.

"Well," he said, trying to stall for time. "I feel like I had to fill it with a hundred other little things to make up for the fun we used to have."

Liv rolled her eyes. "Riiiight. How's the packaging business going?"

"Good. We just signed a new contract with a larger company out of New Hampshire, and…" He stopped and caught himself. "Sorry, you probably don't want to hear about all the details."

She shrugged her shoulders. "I've learned a lot from listening to Ella go on about her marketing techniques. I think it's interesting to learn about different aspects of business. Sometimes I wonder if things would have been different had my father taught us a few more things about what he did for a living."

Dawson could hear the sadness in her words, and he could only imagine what his life would have been like had his father not taken him under his wing and coached him along. The surprise returned as he realized she didn't mind him talking about business. It was somewhat refreshing, as most people didn't have time to listen to what he had to say, away from the office anyway.

"Jeremy opened up one of our facilities over in Southern California, which makes it easier to spread the Holt brand." He grinned at the thought of his younger brother probably still comparing the West and East Coasts, just like he'd done every time the Holts had gone on a trip to California.

"Wow, Ella didn't tell me that. How long ago did he move there?"

"Just a few weeks. He's got the first setup done, and he'll be back in a week or so, staying until the wedding. Then he'll move there permanently." He watched the twitch of her mouth as she thought about that.

"Will that be hard? Having him so far away?"

Taking a minute to think about it, Dawson finally answered, "Yes. Jeremy and I have gotten close in the last few years. I'll miss just walking down the hall at the office to bounce ideas off him."

"You're losing Ella and Jeremy. That's got to be tough." She reached out and placed her hand on his forearm, causing a slight buzz to tingle his skin where her fingers touched.

"I hadn't really thought of it like that. Thanks a lot!" he said, feigning sadness.

The look on her face told him she'd just realized what

she'd said. "I'm so sorry. I didn't mean to make you feel bad. I —the thoughts just tumbled out."

Dawson waved his hand in the air. "You're fine. It's true though. I would have had to face that eventually. Why not now?"

Liv turned to look out into the ocean, her long blond hair trailing behind her from the motion of the ferry. The curve of her chin and the fullness of her lips reminded him of the last time they'd been on Nantucket together. He could still feel the eruption in his chest as they'd kissed on the board-walk near the lighthouse, one of her favorite places to visit, especially near sunset.

"Dawson?" Liv stared at him, and he didn't know what it was about.

"Sorry, what?"

"How is your mother?"

He thought about it for a few seconds. "She's good. She's easing into retirement by traveling through Europe. You knew she got remarried, right?"

She nodded, raising an eyebrow before saying, "That's a good thing, right?"

"Yeah, her husband is a good guy. He balances out her intensity, which we're all happy about. I feel bad saying it, but it's nice to be able to control the company how I want. My mother has some great ideas, and she did a great job in my father's absence; there are just things that need changing, and it's easier when I don't have to jump through hoops to do it."

She smiled, her bright white teeth gleaming in the sun. "I can understand that. Hoops are not the most fun thing to deal with, especially when you know the potential of something."

Dawson wasn't quite sure what to say. He gazed out at the horizon, the island only a few hundred yards out. They'd been together on the ferry for just over an hour, and yet it had felt like minutes. A strange sensation flowed through him, as though they hadn't missed a moment since that summer four years ago. What would it be like with two months together?

Just as he thought it, Dawson shook his head. He wasn't here for the summer like old times. He was lucky to get a weekend away from the office as it was. A whole summer was out of the question. And yet as he looked at her, conflicting feelings arose. He wouldn't mind spending more time with her. Adelyn had never been this easy to talk to nor had she understood things as quickly as Liv did. Two different women, but his heart was already picking a side.

CHAPTER 7

Once the ferry docked at Nantucket, a sense of anxiety squeezed Olivia's chest. There was so much about this place that brought back all the old memories. The smell of fish and cobblestones everywhere. The buzz of energy from people milling around the dock. Not only that, she could already sense the slower pace.

She'd missed it. She knew as hard as it might be nannying in the home she'd come to for over two decades of summers, maybe she needed this experience to finally move on.

It almost felt like Nantucket was the last good place left before her life careened out of control. The fear that maybe she'd put it on a pedestal as the source of her past happiness crept in.

"Ella is right there. Let me take those for you." She turned to see where Dawson pointed. He shifted his duffel bag over his shoulder and took the two rolling suitcases from her, their fingers grazing just the littlest bit and causing heat to shoot up her arms.

What was her problem? She'd never had issues with

blushing this much around anyone before, even Dawson. Why now?

Maybe because his cologne reminds you of that night.

There was that. And his eyes, a milky chocolate color that she could swim in for days, did nothing to help the situation. But now wasn't the time to be thinking about that. She had a job to do, one that would help her family survive a few more weeks, no matter what came their way.

Olivia followed Dawson to the car, and Ella got out of the SUV, hugging Olivia and punching Dawson on the shoulder.

"Looks like you two got to ride over together, huh? Did you do a lot of catching up?" She wriggled her eyebrows in teasing, and Olivia tried to get her to stop with a quick shake of the head.

Giving Dawson a sideways glance, Olivia said, "Yep. Where are we going for dinner? I'm so hungry."

The three of them laughed, walking to the back to load up the luggage and then hopping into the SUV. Olivia had taken the passenger seat since no one had been on her side, but she was surprised to find Dawson next to her in the driver's seat, with Ella right behind him.

"Should we go to the diner?" he asked, locking his eyes with hers.

Feeling breathless, she said, "Yeah." With a quick pause, she raised her voice and said, "I haven't had one of their shakes in so long. Do they still do the cherry chocolate chip?"

Dawson scrunched his nose in disgust. "I forgot you liked that disgusting combination. You need to stick with the mint chocolate chip, or mint Oreo. Those are way better." He grinned, a twinkle in his eye reminding her he was teasing.

"Have you ever tried it? I remember you avoiding it at all costs."

"Cherries. They just ruin good food." Dawson pretended to gag.

Ella tapped the back of the seat and said, "Now, now. Am I going to have to separate you two?"

With that, Olivia felt sixteen again, back to the same old playful banter she'd always shared with Dawson. There was a small thread of difference, as though things could never be the same after that wonderful kiss four years ago. But as long as she could figure things out in the next couple of months, maybe she'd have a chance to move on with her life, and not stay stuck hoping for what she'd had in the past.

* * *

THE FOOD at their favorite diner didn't disappoint. The place hadn't changed a bit; the wall in their favorite booth still had their names scratched into it from when the girls were thirteen.

"Okay, here's the moment of truth. Taste this." Olivia held out the spoon, the pinkish ice cream with small flecks of chocolate threatening to drip onto the table below. She leaned over the table and placed it right in front of his mouth. "Come on. They use maraschino cherries, so it's not going to taste tart or whatever."

Dawson's eyebrows knitted together, and Olivia had to keep her laugh controlled so the ice cream didn't drop down his shirt. He finally opened his mouth but didn't move any closer, like a young boy forced to eat peas and finally giving in.

Olivia took the chance and shoved the ice cream in, watching his face for each flicker of emotion. His jaw moved forward and back a few times, looking as though he were trying to get it to melt on his tongue, no expression on his face.

"And?" Ella asked, watching just as intently as Olivia.

Pursing out his lips and smacking them together, he said, "It's actually not that bad."

Olivia turned and high-fived Ella, the two of them laughing over the annoyance on Dawson's face.

Draping an arm over the back of the booth, Dawson looked between Ella and Olivia. "What is the plan for the weekend then, girls?"

Olivia turned to Ella, knowing her friend would already have an itinerary.

"We're going to have a girls weekend."

"You're not going to let me hang out with you?" Dawson feigned hurt, and Olivia chuckled.

"What about your weekend of work?" Ella asked, eyebrow raised.

Olivia looked to Dawson for his response and saw the small mental battle going on in his head. She wasn't sure if she wanted him to say he had to work all weekend or that he was open to spend it with them.

"This trip is for relaxation. I might have to do a little work, but I've delegated a lot to the members of my team so I can hang out and take some much needed time off. What have you got in mind?"

"Adelyn won't be gracing us with her presence, will she?" Ella's voice had a hard edge to it, and Olivia was surprised, as she'd never heard that side of her best friend before. She remembered Ella talking about the girl Dawson had been dating for the past two years but since she hadn't seen Dawson in so long, she'd forgotten.

Dawson shook his head, biting his bottom lip and twirling the fork absentmindedly on his plate. "No, we're on a break."

Ella let out a sigh and said, "Finally. I didn't think you'd ever get rid of her."

Olivia had to shove her curiosity down. It wasn't her

place to ask all the questions spinning in her head about Dawson's relationship, and she just needed to focus on what she could. Making up her mind, she would have fun for the weekend and then move on, doing her job and having fun for the rest of the summer.

"How long are you here for?" Olivia asked, focusing on catching the dripping ice cream around the side of her cone. She was more than curious but didn't want to seem over-eager about his presence. Whatever she'd done, she felt more awkward in his presence now, and she hoped it wouldn't make for an embarrassing summer.

"The weekend for now. We'll see how things go from there." He gave her a cockeyed smile, setting her insides racing.

"We'll have to make the most of it then, won't we?" She gave him a coy smile, trying not to feel the shock of her words. This guy was more adorable than she remembered. It was probably good she wasn't staying at the Holt home longer than the weekend, or she might not be able to break the spell he slowly spun around her, whether he knew it or not.

CHAPTER 8

Getting ready for bed later, Ella came and fell on Olivia's bed.

"What's up?" Olivia asked, bouncing down by her friend.

"Just got off the phone with Tony." She let out a sigh and said, "I miss that boy."

Olivia laughed and shook her head. "The last time I saw him, he definitely wasn't a boy." She pictured the tall, sandy-blond guy Ella had fallen in love with the summer before. He was an inch shorter than Dawson and built about the same, but the similarities stopped there.

"Yeah, well, I'm still waiting to hear you say you've fallen madly in love with someone. Now that things didn't work out with *The Suitor*, are you going to finish out the matching process?"

Sighing, Olivia fell back on the bed, staring up at the white ceiling, doing her best not to think about Dawson. "I don't know, Ella. I mean, it feels kind of odd to hope that someone will be a good match for you if someone else picked them out. Especially after the show."

"Yeah, but you were in the envelope. That means you had a high chance of falling for Carson."

Shaking her head, Olivia said, "Once I found out Ruby was the one who'd had a relationship with him before, I knew I couldn't stand in the way of that."

Ella nodded. "So, you let her have him." It was more of a statement of fact than a question, and Olivia knew it was true.

"Not consciously at first, but by the end, I knew we could be friends. I just couldn't see her having to live a life without him."

"Carson is a good guy. He and Dawson have been friends for a while, and he's not at all what the media says about him."

"You're so right about that," Olivia said.

There was a pause, letting her breathe in and out a few times before Ella dug a little deeper.

"So, who's to say that when you're officially matched, you wouldn't have a chance? Look at Meg, the matchmaker, and Parker. Brennen and Lexie. Carson and Ruby. All these people are finding the love of their life while connected to Love, Austen. Why not you?"

There's only one I'd be interested in, but he's got his own relationship issues.

Olivia turned to look at Ella, who was inspecting her fingernails. "What's the story with Dawson and Adelyn? You don't sound like you're a fan."

"She's nice enough, she just rubs me the wrong way. Dawson proposed to her a month ago." Ella paused, giving Olivia a look that conveyed her irritation. Olivia's heart beat against her ribcage. He was more serious about the girl than she'd thought.

"And?" Olivia hoped she'd hurry up and spill the rest of the story. She didn't know how much suspense she could take when it came to Dawson's relationship. Maybe knowing the whole story would stop her heart from feeling anything more than a schoolgirl crush.

Ella made a face, and said, "She hasn't given him an answer. I think that's why they're on a break." She accentuated the last word with air quotes, and Olivia frowned. If even Ella didn't think they were done with the relationship, Olivia couldn't get her hopes up.

"What now?" Olivia asked, sitting up. "She hasn't given him an answer, after a month? Is she crazy?"

"I know, right? Who does that? Dawson told me a week ago he's been trying to give her some space so she can decide. I told him that if it's not a yes by now, he might as well move on. There are plenty of girls willing to love on him." She stared into Olivia's eyes, a slight smile forming. "Maybe this break will be good for him. He can see what he's been missing out on."

"Ain't that the truth," Olivia said, breathless. "That's just—I can't understand what she's thinking. He's one of the kindest people out there, and being a CEO, it's difficult to keep that image. Besides, he's not bad on the eyes."

With an elbow to the side, Ella said, "If I didn't know better, I'd say you still held a torch for him."

Trying to show nonchalance, Olivia said, "Well, he'll always be the guy I compare other ones to, probably because I've known him forever."

"I signed him up for Love, Austen too."

Whipping her head in Ella's direction, Olivia studied her face, wanting to see if she was serious or not.

"You didn't."

With a nod and a mischievous grin, Ella said, "Yep. I wanted him to know that Adelyn isn't the only option out there, that there are a lot of other women out there he could click with."

Afraid to be too eager, she asked, "Did he do it?"

"I don't know. But I think I'll put a bug in his ear and get him to take the tests at least. Then he can get the results of his top three matches and decide from there."

"I'm excited to see your persuasive methods on this one." Olivia knew Ella was good at a lot of things, persuasion being one of them. But when it came to matters of her brother's heart, would he listen?

Standing and stretching, Ella winked at her. "What should we do tomorrow? We've got to make the most of this weekend before you start working, girl."

"Which means sleep would be good. I'm not eighteen again where I can stay out all night and be semi-coherent the next day."

"You read my mind exactly. Eleven isn't early by any means, but it's not our old hours. I'll see you in the morning."

Ella left Olivia to her thoughts, which seemed to swirl like a blizzard. She couldn't fathom not jumping at the chance to marry someone like Dawson. He'd be not only a great partner but an amazing father. She'd seen him with kids, and it always warmed her heart how sweet he was with them.

Don't get your hopes up too high, Liv. There's a lot that can or can't happen in the next few months.

A part of her felt bad at the glimmer of hope she held that Dawson wouldn't take Adelyn back, allowing Olivia to somehow find a way back to where they'd begun four years earlier. Just to see if there were any possibilities before she completely gave up her dream of Dawson by her side. There was a possibility they could be matched, but the thought of him matching with three other girls who weren't her made her more anxious than she should feel about a guy who would never be hers.

After a late night of trying to forget about Dawson, Olivia woke up later than usual, feeling more refreshed than she had in weeks. Sadly, the guest bed at the Holt summer home was a lot more comfortable than her lumpy mattress at home. She showered and threw on a pair of shorts and a t-shirt, not sure what to wear since they hadn't decided what they were doing just yet.

As she walked into the main room just off the kitchen, she saw Dawson turned toward the fridge, pulling out a carton of juice. The t-shirt he wore accentuated the strong build of his back, pulling tight across the muscles in his arms. He wore a pair of Star Wars pajama pants, and she couldn't help but smile.

"Morning," she said, leaning against the countertop of the island.

Dawson jumped, spilling drops of juice on his shirt as he turned around. "Morning." He gave her a wide grin before pulling a napkin from the counter and wiping at the spots of juice. "I didn't hear you walk in."

"I work in stealth mode as much as possible. Sometimes

it's nice to fly under the radar." As much as she tried to give him a genuine smile, it hit her how much that comment resonated with her. She'd been flying under the radar for so long. Figuring out a life where she had to be the breadwinner was more than scary.

It wasn't like *The Suitor* was an international success, but she was surprised that she hadn't been stopped at least once or twice and asked about it. In the week she'd been home, no one had even mentioned it. Maybe the show wasn't as big of a hit as the producers made it out to be.

"I can imagine that's nice. Probably easier than being recognized as part of the Holt family. Did you and Ella decide what you're up to today?" He lifted the cup of juice to his lips, eyebrow raised.

Olivia shook her head. "Not yet. I'm just waiting for Sleeping Beauty to make an entrance."

"Well, then you've got another hour or two to wait. Do you want a bagel?" He pulled his out of the toaster and spread strawberry cream cheese over it.

"Sure. I can throw one in."

He waved his hand and pointed to the seat at the bar. "I don't cook much, but a bagel and cream cheese is something I can't mess up. Just relax."

She felt the nerves surge up through her and pulled her phone out, checking messages and emails. The only new emails she'd gotten were for sales at different stores. No headline saying, "You're hired!" or "We'd like an interview."

Footsteps echoed down the hall, and Olivia looked up to see Ella strolling into the kitchen.

"Sparky's Sports World."

"Huh?" Olivia and Dawson echoed at the same time.

Ella grinned even wider, her eyes sparkling with mischief. "We should go to Sparky's today. We haven't been back in a few summers, and it would be the perfect way to kick off this summer."

Olivia put her hand on her hip. "You do know that it's not the start of summer, right?"

Unaffected, Ella said, "So? It's the beginning of Holt and Justice fun, until Holt becomes Mrs. Spencer." She squealed and disappeared back down the hall.

Dawson handed Olivia the bagel on a paper towel and took a bite of his own. After a few bites, he said, "I should probably go change if I'm going to beat you at go-karts today." He tried to give her an intimidating stare, but it only sent Olivia into a fit of laughter.

"What? You don't want to summon the force with those pants?"

He looked down, and a slight blush covered his cheeks. "As much as I like Star Wars, no. That's all I'd need. A front-page picture of me in my pajamas." His eyes twinkled as he walked away, taking another bite of bagel as he left.

That cute half-grin sent her heart pumping and her stomach flipping. Why wasn't she over him by now? If she could tell her ten-year-old self she'd still have a huge crush on Dawson seventeen years later, she probably would've laughed at the thought. The worst part is she'd thought those feelings would fade over time. But they only seemed to grow stronger, and she was headed for a heartbreak.

Thinking of Sparky's, the excitement she'd felt summer after summer of going there bubbled up inside her. She had some old scores to settle on the mini-golf course and a streak to protect on the go-karts. Dawson might be the guy of her dreams, but this was the one thing she wouldn't be letting him win.

CHAPTER 10

Sparky's Sports World was one of the things Dawson loved most about the island. He remembered his father taking him with Ella and Jeremy several times over the course of their childhood. A few years ago, he'd seen signs of construction around the building. They'd added a newer front entrance and fresh paint throughout, as well as a few new attractions. Walking through the front gates now, he had the same sense of wonder and excitement as he had twenty years or more ago.

"Three all-day passes, please." He smiled at the young girl working the ticket window.

"Okay, great. All adults?" The girl pulled out a book and flipped some pages, stopping on one. She slid her finger down the page and stopped at one line. He grunted, and she said, "Three adults. Everything Pass. That will be sixty-nine fifty." The girl smiled and waited as Dawson removed a card from his wallet.

Sliding it over, he pulled the neon-pink wristbands from under the glass and tore them apart, handing one to Ella and

Olivia before wrapping one around his own wrist and securing it.

The line extended behind them, and looking through the metal gate to the park, Dawson could already see a large group of people milling about. He should've been used to crowds, having to weave through them every day to get to work in downtown Boston, but when it was something for fun, he just wished everyone would go home and leave the park to the three of them.

Clapping his hands together, he asked, "Where should we start?'

Ella grinned wildly and said, "Let's start with the go-karts. I'm ready to see the rematch you've been wanting for the last few years." She nudged Dawson, and he laughed.

Olivia's face showed her confusion. "Rematch you've wanted for years? No one told me about this. I would've made a special trip over here just to beat you had I known about this silent wish." Her laugh filled him with ease, and he realized how much he'd missed it.

"I don't know about that, Blondie. That track is mine."

They turned to walk around the mini-golf course, and he took in the smells of burned rubber and popcorn wafting through the air. All of it brought back a deep feeling of nostalgia, and he wanted to cling to it all longer. As much as he loved his job, being here was just a sign that he needed to delegate more on the things he could at the office. He was still young, but his father had basically died from overworking himself, and Dawson didn't want to follow in those footsteps.

The attendant at the go-karts instructed them to stand at the gate and wait, as several carts already wound around the small course.

Dawson turned to Olivia and said, "Are you ready for this?"

She laughed, her eyes almost shut in the process. "Yup. I'm ready to continue my streak as the defending champion."

The attendant made a face and leaned in, whispering loudly to Ella, "I take it these two have a history on the go-karts?"

"My friend is the reigning champion, if I remember correctly." Ella's pronunciation was accentuated as she looked at Dawson.

The young man held out his hand in a fist, and Olivia pounded hers against it. "I like it."

"She cheats." Dawson turned to look directly at Liv, his eyebrows raised in challenge.

"I do not. I just happened to say that I thought I saw Tom Brady walking by last time. That wasn't cheating." She giggled, and Dawson shook his head, trying to keep a smile from his face and failing.

"You know how much I've always wanted to meet him. That wasn't fair." He pretended to pout, and Liv touched his upper arm, sending tingles rippling up through his shoulder.

She shook her head. "You've always been too big-headed anyway. We had to find a way to take down the champion of everything else." Her eyes stared into his, a sparkle there that captivated him. A current moved between the two of them, and the attraction he'd been feeling for Olivia the past day leapt to another level.

The attendant came to the door and unlocked the metal gate, breaking their trance on one another. Dawson glanced to see his sister on her phone. Probably texting Tony.

"Choose your vehicle and make sure the seatbelts are securely fastened," the attendant said, waving them in. "The helmet strap needs to be snapped on the entire time on the track, or we'll have to stop the ride early."

Olivia pushed past Dawson, gunning for a certain red kart with the number eighteen painted in white on the side.

Dawson took up a spot in the car next to her, pulling the helmet on. It took a few tries to get it on his head, and the attendant finally had to punch it down, causing Dawson's ears to burn from lack of room. He buckled the seatbelt and moved the steering wheel back and forth, leaning forward as he looked at Liv. He could only see her eyes dancing as she sat back and waited to begin.

The attendant directed them to the starting line. Dawson and Olivia were lined up in front, Ella stuck behind them with some of the other riders.

The young man pulled out a green flag and waved it. Liv slammed her foot on the gas and took off, Dawson doing the same and moving just behind her. It took one lap for him to remember the layout of the small course but soon enough, he was neck and neck with her. And then with one move, he turned the wheel, pushing her into the wall. He laughed as he saw her eyes wild with competition as he drove by.

With only two laps to go, he was confident he would regain his title of champion go-kart racer when a red cart whipped past him, Liv waving as she passed. While distracted, he'd hit the back of another kart. Ella turned around and frowned at him.

"Watch where you're going, D."

His eyes focused on the red cart. "I am," he mumbled low enough that his sister couldn't hear him. It had been way too long since he'd done something like this, and the fact that Liv was playing along made him feel a connection he'd never felt with Adelyn. With a quick maneuver to the right, he made it past her and did his best to catch up to Liv, the adrenaline of competition pumping through him.

He was only a length back on the end of the last lap and as much as he pushed the pedal to the bottom of the kart, it wouldn't go any faster, allowing Liv to win.

She got out of the kart and beamed, waving her hands in

the air and pretend bowing to an invisible crowd. Stopping his kart next to hers, he took off the helmet and unbuckled the seatbelt, standing on the blacktop. Taking in a breath to swallow his pride, he walked up to Liv and stuck out his hand

"Well-played, Justice. Well-played." She shook his hand and let out a cackle, causing him to smile. Seeing her happiness, he leaned forward and placed a kiss on her cheek. She stilled, looking at him through wide eyes as he stepped back.

Liv's hand slid to her cheek, and she said, "What was that for?"

With a quick shrug of his shoulders, Dawson said, "I don't know. I thought that's what the winner usually gets for these kinds of things." He couldn't read her expression and hoped he hadn't overstepped his bounds. A feeling drew him to her, like an invisible attachment that seemed to shorten every time he was around her.

The two of them were behind the gate, waiting for Ella to arrive a few minutes later. "Geez, you two. I can't believe you crashed into me, Dawson."

"You didn't." Liv's lips curved up as she looked at him for confirmation, her hand on his upper arm, her skin soft.

"I might have been surprised by a certain red go-kart flying past me. Did you have the guy rig it for you or something?" he asked as they weaved through the bars and out to a main pathway through the park.

"No, I'm just that good." She winked at him and turned to Ella. "Mini golf next?"

"Let's do it."

Dawson watched them walking away and tried to get a read on his emotions. His arm tingled where she'd touched. A memory popped up in his mind, the simple kiss he'd shared with Liv before everything changed for the two of them four years ago. That summer had been one of the best in his life, but then his own father had put him through a rigorous training to be CEO before his own passing two years before.

What could have happened between the two of them had their lives not changed so abruptly? Maybe this was their chance to find out.

CHAPTER 11

It had felt good to beat Dawson. No, it was amazing. Just to see the look on his face afterward was well worth it. When he shook her hand, she felt sparks skipping up her arm. And when he'd kissed her on the cheek, she could've sworn that fireworks had been set off.

Cool it, girl. He proposed to someone already.

Dawson retrieved the balls and putters from the attendant at the booth. He gave Ella the light blue and kept an orange ball, reaching out to hand a red one to Olivia. "Is this still your favorite color?" Her breath caught in her throat, and all she could do was nod. She accepted the ball and putter with a thin smile, electricity jumping between their fingers.

That wasn't something she needed right now, to acknowledge the renewed crush she'd had for so long. She ignored the fact that those old feelings had resurfaced with a vengeance. She was on Nantucket for a job, not start with a broken heart. If she kept hanging out with Dawson, that's what would end up happening. She'd have to find ways to avoid him for the time he was there. After today, of course.

The three of them walked over to the first hole, and Ella set her ball down first. She swung back and knocked the ball down the path and through the hole of the mountain that blocked the hole on the other side. Olivia could feel Dawson standing next to her but resisted the temptation to look over at him.

"How are your mom and sister doing? I haven't seen them in a while." His voice was deep, like chocolate syrup, and she waited for him to keep talking before realizing he was waiting for her answer.

Olivia bit her upper lip, trying to decide how to respond to that. She hadn't told many people about her mother's condition, mostly because she wasn't sure how to react to the pity when they found out. Ella had always been there, especially on the days when she needed to cry a moment. Olivia could handle a lot, but there were times when her world of problems seemed like a mountain she needed to climb rather than a small hill to get to the good stuff.

"Scarlett is good. I just found out she's been dating some doctor." Dr. Turner seemed like the typical charmer and what was worse, that was Scarlett's type to a T. She just hoped her sister wouldn't end up with a broken heart.

"And your mom? Is she still baking away? I think some of my favorite memories are coming over and her handing me a fresh-baked cookie or treat." His face lit up at the thought.

She gave him a sad smile before moving forward to put her ball down. "She, uh, she has Alzheimer's." Her mouth opened to say more, but she found the words wouldn't come, her throat constricting as the threat of tears surfaced. She looked down and hit the ball with her putter. It bounced off the board and rolled back to her. Symbolic of how her life was going right now.

Olivia felt a hand on her upper arm and turned to see

Dawson only a few inches from her. "I'm sorry, Liv. I didn't know. I promise, I didn't."

"You're fine. I swore Ella to secrecy and haven't told many people." She took in a deep breath, focusing on hitting the ball again. This time, it went through the opening, and she breathed a sigh of relief she didn't have to be completely humiliated in front of him.

She joined Ella on the small bit of green below. Dawson's ball came rolling down the pathway and nearly went in the hole, spinning around the rim of it before shooting a few feet away. He walked down and tapped it in, making it look effortless. After pulling it out of the hole, he held it in the air and waved, as if he were on an actual golf course.

"You're such a spaz," Ella said, trying to get her ball to go in several times.

Dawson's face turned sober, and he asked, "How long has it been since she was diagnosed?"

"Almost four years. Just a few months after my father's funeral." Her words made him flinch, and she wondered what had caused it.

"And what do the doctors say? Is she doing okay for now?" With his milky brown irises staring at her, Olivia's knees wobbled, but hopefully not enough to notice.

Ella finally hit the ball into the hole and grabbed it out. "What's with all the questions? Leave the poor girl alone."

Olivia raised a hand and said, "It's fine. You guys are like my family anyway. I went in with Scarlett the day after I got home from the show, and the doctor said she is showing signs of moderate dementia. The original diagnosis said she was expected to live anywhere from three to ten years, some people living longer than that. With this news, I'm not sure if that will cut down how much time she has left or not."

"Does she still recognize you?" Dawson asked, focused on

the ball in his hand. Ella made a fist and punched him in the shoulder, causing Olivia to laugh hard.

He rubbed at the spot and frowned at Ella. "What was that for?"

"For being insensitive."

"She just said we're like family. Families share things so they can comfort one another." He turned back toward Olivia and gave her a look of reassurance before moving to the next hole.

Family. Right. Nothing like feeling foolish for overanalyzing every action and emotion since she'd found him on the ferry. He probably thought of her like a little sister.

Olivia putted first this time, with Dawson behind her. When they moved down to the next section of the hole, she turned to him and said, "Yesterday was the first day she's recognized me in months. I went to see her before I got on the ferry. She called me Livvy and then said something about bringing my dolls to Nantucket."

A burning sensation formed in her throat, and Olivia didn't think she'd be able to hold back the tears this time. Without a word, Dawson wrapped his arms around her and pulled her close. His arms formed a protective barrier, allowing her to feel that everything would work out, if only for a few seconds. The problems that plagued her elsewhere seemed to be lighter, as if he could take on some of the burden.

She wrapped her arms around his waist and waited a few seconds, breathing in the scent of a clean breeze from his cologne. It was tempting to stay in his arms longer, but if he was still dating someone, she wasn't about to be a relationship wrecker. But she was also profoundly grateful for his comfort.

"Thank you. It's amazing what a hug can do, huh?" She

forced a smile as she stepped back, then used her fingertips to wipe away some of the moisture that had escaped.

Ella stood next to Dawson. "Just know we're here for you. No matter what, we'll help you through it."

Olivia thought of the expensive bills and everything she'd been faced with the past few years. The sentiment and the friendship from the Holts was something she needed right now, and she just might be able to keep moving forward.

CHAPTER 12

The weekend had gone by much faster than Dawson had expected, but it was better than he could've thought. The three of them had spent most of Sunday hanging out, watching movies and playing games at the big house. He'd debated whether to head back to Boston Sunday night but decided to stay until Monday morning.

By the time he got up that morning, the sun was up higher than he was used to. All the early morning conference calls with people from different countries and time zones meant he was used to waking up while it was still dark, and the brightness made him feel off.

He glanced out the window and over to the large six-car garage attached to the main house, with the cottage sitting right next to it. Soon enough, all the rooms on the property would be filled with family or friends, here to celebrate Ella's wedding to Tony. Ella had done so many measurements over in what the family called the Pavilion, Dawson was surprised it wasn't already decorated for the festivities two short months away.

He sat on the bed, Liv's words echoing in his mind. *You're losing them both at the same time.*

It was hard to think about since Ella and Jeremy were the two people he went to with most of his decisions. How would he survive being the only person to stay put while the rest of his family ran off to different parts of the world? Was that why he'd been pushing so hard for an engagement to Adelyn? Was he ready for a commitment like that?

All he knew was that he didn't want to be alone.

Dressing in a pair of slacks and a nicer polo shirt, he packed up his duffel bag and walked out to the kitchen. Ella sat at the bar alone, drinking her usual morning orange juice while reading the newspaper. When she sat there like that, she reminded him more and more of their father. It had been his routine to read the paper from front to back every morning before heading out for work.

"You the only one up?"

"No, Olivia is already at the Bourdens'. Who's Sleeping Beauty now?" Ella said with a grin.

Dawson stretched and yawned, feeling a pop in his back. "Yeah, but I think I needed it after hanging out with you two all weekend." He grinned at her, and she laughed back. "Are you planning on coming to the office this week?"

Ella spooned some cereal into her mouth and shook her head. Dawson poured a glass of milk while he waited for her to chew and swallow.

"No, I can do everything I need to from here. I'm surprised you're running back to the city. I haven't seen you as relaxed as you are right now in, well, years. At least since Mom handed the company over to you."

"That's what happens when you're CEO."

Giving him a face, she said, "It's possible to delegate, you know. You try to do it all by yourself. That's not healthy."

"How do you think we got the company to where it is

today?" Dawson leaned forward across the island, only a few inches from her face until she looked up at him.

She rolled her eyes and said, "I'll give you that. But don't you want to have a life? There are so many qualified candidates that work for our company. Use them and their talents. Stop micromanaging them, and you'll free up time for yourself." Using her spoon, she dunked the cereal below the milk. "But Angela isn't one of them. How have you survived her sucking up to you all the time?"

Dawson chuckled, the statement reminding him of his conversation with Barbara days earlier. "Very carefully, I guess. And it might shock you to know that I'm working on delegating. Barbara has pointed it out on several occasions, and this weekend was a small test run." He took another sip of milk and said, "Maybe I'll come more often this summer. This has been a good break, and I could use some more."

"This could be the Holt Home Office for the summer," she said with a wink.

Nodding, Dawson drank his milk in three large gulps, rinsing out the cup and setting it into the dishwasher. "What do you want me to get you for your wedding?"

"For you to bring a date that isn't named Adelyn Garrett." Ella's straight face told him volumes about her feelings toward his sort of ex-girlfriend.

He paused for a moment, an idea playing out in his head. "What would you think if I took those tests?"

Ella bent the newspaper enough to see him, her expression serious. "Are we talking about the matchmaking tests?"

Dawson nodded. "I told Adelyn we were on a break, but I think I'm just done. It's time I find someone to settle down with. Is that bad?" With anyone else, Dawson would have felt awkward talking about it, but with Ella, it was just another topic of discussion, one he knew she'd been hoping he'd talk to her about for months now.

Slapping the newspaper on the countertop, Ella grinned. "Are you kidding? I think it's great! You deserve to find someone who makes you happy for the long term. Adelyn won't make you happy."

The comment stung, as if Ella didn't trust his judgment when it came to love. As he thought about women he'd dated before Adelyn, she'd always been supportive. It must have just been Adelyn she didn't care for.

"I can find them online, right?" When she nodded yes, he said, "Well, I'll fill them out tonight then." The thought of being matched with some strangers sent a shred of doubt through him, but maybe a few dates would help him find a girl who would be good for him. His mind strayed, showing him a picture of Olivia with that brilliant smile. He shook his head, knowing she probably thought of him as a brother.

Making his way around the counter, he kissed his sister on the forehead and said, "Okay, I'm heading to the ferry. Do you want to drop me off or are you planning to walk for the rest of the week?"

"I'll drive you. Maybe one of those next free days you're out here, you can get the old car working again. It would be nice to have another one on the island."

"We need to bring one out, especially for the wedding. That could be nuts trying to shuttle everyone here."

They walked out to the garage, and he glanced over to the old car their father had purchased when Dawson was fourteen, in the hopes they could rebuild it together. They'd made some progress before he died a decade later, but Dawson never had the heart to work on it again.

"Maybe," was all he said. He pulled open the driver's side door and got in, trying to stop the tidal wave of memories.

* * *

MAKING it to the office just after lunch, Dawson wasn't sure he was ready to be back to the grind. Barbara came in within three minutes of his arrival with a list of missed calls.

"How was your weekend?" she asked, looking him over as if she were his grandmother.

"It was really good. Refreshing."

The older woman smiled and said, "Good. Did you do anything fun?"

"Just hung out with Ella and Liv."

"Liv Justice? How is she doing?" Barbara's voice took on a tone of pity, and Dawson now understood what Liv had meant when she didn't want to tell the world about her mother's condition. There was enough pity from the death of her father and the change in fortune.

Smiling, he said, "She's doing well. She's nannying for the family next door this summer, which I think will be good for Ella. With Mom gone to Europe for the next month, at least she'll have someone there if she needs anything."

Barbara gave him a sad look. "You've been head of this family for too long. You need someone who can balance you out and make it so you don't take on the burden of everything."

"You're just rooting against Adelyn, aren't you?" he said, more playfully than he intended. "Sounds like Ella feels the same."

"I just want what's best for you. I've been with this company long enough to be your second mother, or grand-mother even. I want to see you happily settled."

Leaning forward, Dawson said, "Is there someone you had in mind besides Miss Garrett?"

"Oh, I have a list, but I'll let you figure out your love life on your own. Right now, we've got a fire to put out with our shipping department in Manchester."

Turning his mind back to work, Dawson wondered about

Barbara's words. Balance. What would that person look like? Olivia's face popped into his mind. She made him laugh and was strong, even with the things that had been thrown her way. Her beauty didn't hurt either.

The phone rang, and he shook his head, knowing he needed to get back to work. He'd have to sort out his love life later. Maybe taking those tests would help.

CHAPTER 13

Olivia hadn't slept well the night before, knowing that the next morning she'd have to face the home that was no longer hers. She wheeled her luggage down the long driveway of the Holts' property and along the main road until she reached the winding road she'd driven down more times than she could remember.

Taking a deep breath, she strolled up the driveway until she stood about fifty feet away from the front door. The nostalgia she'd experienced just by getting off the ferry was nothing compared to this moment, the memories hitting against her like the waves on the shore. Happy memories, sad occasions, milestones. All the summer memories she could hold seemed to want to take center stage at that moment.

She wasn't sure how long she stood there, but she counted to three and stepped forward, knowing that once she'd entered the home, she could get past the surge of anxiety that had piled up within her.

With both suitcases behind her, she pushed the doorbell, feeling odd to be the one pushing it. She heard running on the other side of the door, and it opened to reveal a young boy and girl, their eyes bright and curious. A woman appeared behind it, her hair the same near-bright white hair as the children's, reflecting the rays of sun that shone through.

"Olivia? It's nice to meet you in person. I don't usually hire someone without having a face-to-face meeting, but Ella assured me you'd be perfect for the job."

With a slight nod, Olivia's eyes turned to the large staircase in front of her, surprised to find the wooden railing changed out for a wood and steel combination. The walls had been painted a different color, and the whole feeling of the place was different. Not a bad different, but Olivia found herself breathe out a sigh of relief. If it had been identical to what she remembered, she might have crumpled into a pile right there.

"Are you all right?" Mrs. Bourden's words pulled Olivia back to the present.

"I'm so sorry. Yes, I'm fine. I, it's just, I have a lot of memories of this house." She moved a hand around as if to encompass everything.

The woman's eyes narrowed. "Memories of this house? We've owned it for—"

"Four years, I know. My parents owned it until my father died, and we had to sell it."

Pressing a hand to her chest, Mrs. Bourden gasped. "Oh my goodness! Ella didn't say you were a Justice. Or maybe she did, and it didn't register. Will you be okay working here?"

Giving her first genuine smile of the morning, Olivia nodded. "I was a little worried about it but seeing the changes you've made, it looks almost like a different house to me. I should be fine." Sitting on her heels, she said, "And these two must be Seth and Rebecca, right?"

Seth folded his arms across his chest and tipped his head back, trying to give her a stern expression. Rebecca giggled and sucked on her thumb.

"These are the twins. Like I said on the phone, they just turned five back in April and will be starting school this coming year. We got them into the Carlington Prep Academy, and they've got a lot to learn to make sure they can stay there, which is one of the focuses for this summer. Let me show you where everything is."

Forty-five minutes later, Olivia had been through the main floor and then the upper. Mrs. Bourden showed her where she would be staying, which turned out to be Scarlett's old room, and where the small classroom had been set up, Olivia's old quarters. She hoped the woman didn't expect them to be inside all day every day. If that were the case, this summer would drag on forever.

"Do you have any questions or requests?"

"I just ask that I have one day every week or two to go to Boston to visit my mother, Mrs. Bourden. She hasn't been doing well health-wise, and I just want to make sure she's all right."

"Of course. We can accommodate that." The woman reached out and rubbed her hand on Olivia's upper arm, trying to be reassuring. The whole scene felt odd, since Mrs. Bourden was only a year older than Olivia at most. "Please call me Shaylee. When I get called Mrs. Bourden, I feel like people are referring to my mother-in-law." She grinned, and Olivia felt a little more at ease.

"I can do that."

"When it comes to family functions, you'll be attending anything we have with my husband's family. As for my family, my mother doesn't agree with having a nanny, and so you won't have to come with us to events on my side. Don't worry, we'll still pay you, it just gets a bit more complicated than I'd like."

Olivia smiled. "You're fine. I can understand not wanting to rock the boat too much."

Mrs. Bourden's smile conveyed her relief, but for what exactly, Olivia wasn't sure. "Well, I need to run some errands, so I will be back this afternoon. Jane is our cook, and she'll be arriving within the next few hours to get dinner started. You'll find some things for lunch in the fridge, and the keys to the car are on the hook by the door to the garage. Let me know if you need help finding anything, and I'll see you later." Shaylee bent over and gave her kids a hug before dashing out the door.

Turning to look at the two kids, Olivia hunched back down. "Okay, kids. What should we do today?"

Rebecca frowned. "We're supposed to do our studies." The thumb came out long enough for her to say that and popped back in.

"Well, what if we have a reward for doing our studies? If we get them done before lunch, maybe we can go for a picnic." Both kids bounced with excitement and took off up the stairs, pushing each other on the way up.

Olivia followed behind them with regular steps. The kids seemed to be good and very obedient.

Still curious, she said, "Are you sad your other nanny left?"

"Nah, she didn't like us anymore. She said something about going to live with the guy who always kissed her." Seth's words sounded more uncaring than his face showed, and Olivia wondered why.

Prior to walking in the room set up as a classroom, she had to take a moment. It had once been her room, and there were a lot of differences, lessening the anxiety in her chest somewhat. But the similarities stood out as well—the same windowpane and the same bookshelves on the one wall.

Without thinking about it, she strode over to the window and removed one of the tiles that decorated the small ledge around it. She turned on the flashlight on her phone and shined it into the hole. When she saw there were no bugs or rodents, she stuck her hand in and touched something cold. Pulling it out, her eyes went wide. The circular hoop was a charm bracelet her father had given her for her twelfth birthday. He'd given her an Eiffel tower and a star because he'd always called her his little star. She'd forgotten about it after the funeral, having to hurry and pack up the rest of the house before the Bourdens moved in.

"What is that?" Seth asked, peeking over her shoulder.

"My old charm bracelet. My parents used to own this house, and this was the room I stayed in during the summer. I put it in there and must have forgotten about it."

Rebecca held the bracelet carefully in her palm. "So, this is really old?"

Olivia threw back her head and laughed. "Not that old, girl. But my dad gave it to me."

"Can we stop worrying about some dumb jewelry and get our homework done?" Seth's irritated voice came from the desks. He must have gotten bored after seeing it was only a piece of jewelry.

Focusing on the list of tasks for the kids that day, Olivia said, "Okay, let's get this homework done so we can go play."

After giving the kids instructions, she stared at the bracelet, one of the small miracles of being here. Like getting a small bit of closure after a long few years.

* * *

OLIVIA HAD GONE down and packed a lunch for her and the kids while they finished up their studies. She pulled out a blanket from a pile by the large fireplace in the front room, holding the basket as she leaned against the railing to the stairs.

"Are you all done?" she called up the stairs, antsy to get outside and do something. She wasn't sure how long the mom expected them to stay inside every day, but there was something about Nantucket that made her think she had to be outside all the time, or it would be a waste of a summer.

Footsteps pounded down the stairs, and the excitement on their faces made her smile.

"Where are we going?" Rebecca asked. As she went to put her thumb back in her mouth, Olivia touched her arm.

"We're going outside to a spot I loved as a kid. It will be perfect for a picnic."

The kids jumped up and down as she opened the back door. Once outside, she pointed to the beach down by the pond that bordered the property. There was a copse of trees that the Holt property shared with them, a place where she'd spent so long daydreaming and pretending throughout the years. She flipped the blanket out to sit on the sand and pulled out sandwiches, chips, veggies, and some drinks from the bag she'd found in a closet.

Seth ran around the beach like someone who'd just found freedom, and Rebecca skipped along behind him.

"Hey, you two! Come eat, and then we can go exploring."

Within minutes, the food was devoured. Seth turned to her and asked, "What do we do when we explore?"

Standing, Olivia brushed her hands on her pants, stepping out onto the soft sand. "There are all kinds of exploring. You can just walk along a little slower than normal and find things in the sand. When I was a little older than you, my friends and I found a bunch of pretty shells in this area."

The kids bent over and moved sand back and forth, chatting here and there. The sound for her text messages went off and turning on the phone, she saw Dawson's name. Her heart leapt, and she wondered what he could be contacting her about.

I hope your first day goes well.

She bit her bottom lip, a wave of emotion flowing through her. Bending down, she said to the kids, "Let's take a picture. Say cheese." Seth made a face, and Rebecca smiled around her thumb, both going back to looking through the sand as Olivia sat back and sent Dawson the picture.

Working on teaching them what summer should look like.

Holding onto her phone, her thoughts were across the small stretch of ocean that separated Nantucket from the mainland. If only her crush had gone away years ago, she might not still be holding onto the fantasy of her and Dawson together. But when she thought of her life without him, an ache settled into her chest.

A few minutes later, another message came through, a picture of Dawson pretending to sleep in his office. The yellow polo he wore stood out against his olive skin, and he was even more attractive. She sighed.

"What's wrong, Libiya?" Rebecca asked, leaning over her shoulder. Olivia hadn't heard her approach, and she laughed.

"Just life. This is my friend Dawson. His family lives in the house next door." Olivia pointed in the direction of the Holt property. Rebecca sat on Olivia's lap, settling in.

Tell them this could be their future. Finding shells was the best! Dawson's message said, finally coming through. Her phone was a few years old, and messages took awhile loading.

I'm glad to see you made it back okay. Olivia debated whether to send it. Was it too personal, too serious?

"Come play, girl!" Seth called out to her. She pressed send, stuffing her phone in her back pocket and helping Rebecca stand.

"Let's go play, shall we?" When Rebecca nodded, they ran out onto the beach and walked through the water. This was her job now, and she needed to focus on it, even if the picture of Dawson relaxed in his office chair was now etched into her mind.

CHAPTER 14

Two weeks flew by with all the meetings needed to keep things rolling for the companies they held as clients. Dawson also had to run three of the new client meetings, and he thought about Ella's words. He did work too much, and maybe she was right about delegating more.

Buzzing Barbara on his phone, she answered, "What's up, boss?"

Chuckling, Dawson said, "I think I'm going to head back to Nantucket this afternoon. Do I have any important meetings for next Monday or Tuesday?"

There was a pause on the line, and he could hear her hum. "No. We have that follow-up meeting with the glass company down in Brighton but other than that, just the usual."

"Okay, let's get Carl to take over that meeting as well as any others that pop up. I'm going to take a few days off."

"Glad to hear it, Dawson. Looking at your schedule, you might be able to take off the entire week if you want." He could hear the smile in her voice.

"Are you trying to get rid of me?"

Barbara hung up on him and at first, Dawson wasn't sure

how to feel about it, until the woman stormed through the door.

"I just want you to live longer than your father. So, remember, this is a job and while a lot of us count on its success for a paycheck, that doesn't mean you have to kill yourself to make that happen. Use your employees for the reason you hired them. You might be surprised how much can get done." She grinned at him, as if daring him to challenge her.

Tapping his fingers together, Dawson nodded. "I take it I haven't done enough to delegate? I thought I was doing a good job."

Her lips pursed, as if trying to hold back the rest of the long lecture she'd started when she burst in here.

"No, Dawson," she said, emphasizing each word. "You should be negotiating contracts and holding meetings with the people directly underneath you. There's no reason for you to work with the new clients. That's what your salespeople are for."

Dawson frowned. "That's what my dad always did. He liked to meet with them to get them started out, kind of hook them into using us."

Barbara closed her eyes for a few moments and opened them again. "I know I'm just your secretary, but I've seen a lot over the past thirty years in this company. You learned most of this from your dad, and I just don't want you to regret not taking time for the things that matter. Think about that while you're gone."

From any other person, he might have balked at her words. He was her boss. But she was right in saying that she'd been a part of their family for years, and he knew she only wanted to help.

"Okay, I think I can handle that. You'll make sure my email says I'll be gone and to contact Carl, right?"

"Did you really just ask me that?" Barbara winked at him before nodding. "Get out of here before someone traps you with a hundred questions that someone else can answer for them."

Grabbing his briefcase, Dawson shoved some papers in it along with his laptop and keys to the office. "You're awesome! Thanks, Barb."

"Oh, I almost forgot. A Miss Austen called when you were in the meeting with the Worsters earlier today. She said something about setting up a meeting to go over your results from some tests?" Barb's eyes felt like lasers as she searched every inch of his face for an explanation of what that meant.

Heat raced up and down his back. "Okay, well, if she calls again, tell her I'm out of town, and we'll have to schedule something after."

Walking out the door, he wondered why he'd even taken those tests. Like a formula would tell him who he should live with for the rest of his life. He'd completed them the day he'd returned from Nantucket. He wasn't sure if he'd done it to appease Ella or what, but getting the results meant he'd have to act on them. After two years with Adelyn, a break from dating would be the best thing for him.

And yet he couldn't stop thinking about Olivia. She was his sister's best friend, the girl he'd practically grown up with and one of the people he trusted most in the world. But if he gave into his feelings, would she reciprocate them? Or would their friendship just be weird after that?

He pulled up the messaging app on his phone and opened a new one for Olivia. They'd texted back and forth over the past two weeks, nothing groundbreaking but sharing pictures of what they were doing and chatting here and there.

I'm heading to Nantucket tonight. You and Ella want to meet up for dinner?

He pushed open the large front doors to the office building and bumped into someone before pressing send. Looking up, he apologized and then said, "Adelyn. What are you doing here?"

"I came to surprise you early." When she saw the confused look on his face, she said, "For the show? We've had tickets for months." She held up two paper tickets, and he had to squint to make out the title.

"We're on a break, Adelyn." He rubbed his hands over his face, taking in a deep breath. "Actually I wanted to talk to you about that. I think—"

"Later, Dawson. We're going to be late if we don't go now. And break or not, you bought me the tickets. I want to see the show with you." She gave him the pout face she could probably trademark.

Realizing the date, he nodded, putting his phone away. Adelyn had been dying to see the popular Broadway show, and Dawson had pulled some strings to get tickets for Christmas.

Dawson smiled, bracing himself for another unexpected night with Adelyn. "Just tonight, and then we need to talk." He went through the upcoming months, hoping he hadn't bought anything else that would link him to her for longer. As far as he was concerned, their relationship was over. Maybe tonight would be the opportunity he'd been waiting for to tell her that.

* * *

DINNER HAD GONE WELL. Adelyn talked all about the success she was having with her new marketing ads, and there were moments when Dawson thought she and Ella should sit down together to figure some of this out. He trusted his sister but if there was some extra advice Adelyn was willing to share, why not?

He'd enjoyed the show and was glad he'd gone to it. The singing, the dancing, and the overall production had been amazing, and from what Adelyn said, was as near the original book as could possibly be done.

They left the theater, and Dawson pulled out his phone, turning the volume on again. Olivia's face popped into his mind, and he wondered what she was doing tonight. As he thought about her more and more, the guilt seeped into him. Looking up at Adelyn, he knew he had to tell her tonight. He deserved to find someone who wanted to be with him and for the right reasons, not just have him on her arm to show off, like Adelyn had enjoyed while they were in the theater.

It took over an hour for them to leave the parking garage, and he wished he hadn't listened to her about driving the car home. That was the benefit of transportation in the city—if one train filled up, the next one would be along in five to ten minutes.

Adelyn chatted about the show, and Dawson almost pulled out the breaking up speech three times but decided to wait until he wasn't trapped with her in person for an indeterminate amount of time.

Driving Adelyn home, he looked for the opportunity to ask. Finally, pulling up in front of her apartment out in Cambridge, he touched her forearm, stopping her from getting out of the car.

"I need to say something before you go."

"I am so tired, Dawson. It was such a fun night. Can't it wait until later?"

"No, it can't. We've had a good run, but I'm ready to move on. As much fun as it is to go to events like this, we've been dating for two years, and I need someone I can depend on by my side."

Her lips puckered, and it reminded him of someone eating a lemon. "Dawson, you know I love you. It's just been a rough time lately, and I don't want to rush into anything."

"I'm not asking you to rush into anything. I'm saying that I want to break up. Not just take a break."

Shaking her head, she said, "I don't want that. Can't you just give me some more time?"

With a sigh, Dawson leaned his head on the window, looking out the windshield. "I don't think you'll ever be ready. I proposed six weeks ago, and I get the feeling you don't want anything to change."

"I don't, you're right. It's been so fun going to dinners and events like this. I just don't know if I'm ready for marriage."

"Do you want kids?" Dawson was surprised as the question popped out of his mouth.

She looked at him with her mouth open, more confused than anything. "I guess, one day. Not right this minute, no."

"Well, I do." Something shot through him, a feeling confirming that his head and his heart were saying the same thing. He should have known this from the beginning of their relationship. Whenever they'd talked about the more serious stuff, she'd avoided the questions and hadn't ever fully given him an answer.

He saw the tears form on the bottom of her eyelids, and he had to look away again, not willing to be swayed by it one more time.

"I can't believe you want to break up after a night like this. Why can't you just give me some more time to think about it?" She pulled her lips in, her chin quivering as the tears continued to roll down her face.

Rubbing his hands over his face, Dawson blew out a breath. "You can think about it as long as you want. When you decide, I might not be around."

Her tears stopped short, and the corners of her mouth

turned up slightly. "I can't believe you're breaking up with me over not saying yes to marriage. I'm only twenty-five, Dawson. I still have things I want to do before I settle down."

Frustration ebbed in his chest, and he took a deep breath, hoping to keep his voice even. "Then you should have told me this six weeks ago. Or even months ago. If I'm holding you back from something, now's your chance to go get it." His words grew in volume by the end, his hands waving in the air.

He opened the car door, allowing the air outside to calm him somewhat as he walked around to her side. He opened it for her. Extending his hand, she placed hers in it and stepped out of the car. She wrapped her arms around his waist, and he returned the hug.

"Good luck, Adelyn. I wish you all the best."

She only nodded at him, the corners of her lips pulled down at the sides. He waited for her to go inside before re-entering his car. Driving down the road, he found a spot to park, feeling complete relief. As he reflected over the past six months, he should have been strong enough to break up then. Their relationship had been the same thing over and over again, but he'd been too comfortable to change anything.

Opening his phone, he dialed Ella through Bluetooth as he drove through the winding streets back to his home in Belmont.

"What's up, Dawson?" she said, her voice thick.

"Did I wake you up?"

Ella chuckled. "Not really. I've just been sitting on the couch watching a movie. I got tired after talking to Tony earlier and have been in and out."

He paused a few seconds before continuing. "Everything is okay between you two, right? I don't need to fly to Europe to kick his behind?"

"No," Ella said, laughing hard. "We're good. He's coming out this week until the wedding, so it will be good to be on the same continent again. I've missed him."

The line went silent for a few seconds before she said, "What's wrong? Why are you calling me at almost midnight?"

"I just broke up with Adelyn."

A squeal pierced his ears, and he had to turn the volume down on the radio as the sound echoed in his brain.

"Are you serious right now? That's the best news I've heard in ages. What happened?"

Dawson relayed all the events of the night as Ella sat quiet on the other line. When she spoke, her voice wasn't as excited as he'd expected.

"So, it's not a final breakup?"

"What are you talking about? Yeah, it is. Who waits six weeks to tell the guy who proposed yes or no?" Dawson slammed a fist against the steering wheel.

Ella sighed. "But you're the guy who waited around that long. Dawson, you can't give her any loophole. She'll go have fun for a little bit and then come barging into your life, expecting you to marry her."

A pit formed in Dawson's stomach, and he hoped his sister was wrong about that. Then a thought hit him. "But if I'm in a relationship with someone else, I'll be fine, right?"

"Do you even know who Adelyn is? Remember how she went back to her ex-boyfriend like five times before you two were officially together? You gave her a get out of jail free card."

Pulling up to his house, Dawson pushed the button for his garage door and drove in, turning off the lights once he parked. Leaning his head against the back of the seat, he said, "Ella, I just want to find someone I can talk to, like this. Someone who balances me out."

Ella laughed, and Dawson frowned, not sure what she was laughing about. "You've been talking to Barbara."

"How'd you know?"

"Because I talk to her," Ella said, her voice sounding more triumphant than Dawson wanted. "That's exactly what she told me when we were talking about you the other day."

Irritation spread through him. "Traitor."

"I'm a meddling sister. I just want you to be happy, like I am with Tony."

Dawson paused, trying to gauge his feelings. He hadn't been happy, not happy, with Adelyn. She'd liked the idea of their relationship, only calling when she wanted to go somewhere. Bitterness swept over him. He'd let that happen, thinking she didn't complain about his work schedule, so it must have been okay. It should've been her who confronted him about working too much, not his sister and his secretary.

"We don't always get the fairytale ending, Ells."

"Don't give up just yet." She didn't say anything for a minute and then asked, "Are you coming to Nantucket this weekend?"

"Yeah."

"Good. You could use some time away from the city. Come hang out with Liv and me."

He didn't want to say how much he wanted to do just that. His feelings for his sister's best friend were still unclear, but he knew he liked being around her.

"I'll text you when I get on the ferry tomorrow. Plan something for us to do."

"Don't worry about that. I'll have everything ready."

Her tone sent a pang of worry to his chest. What did she have up her sleeve?

CHAPTER 15

Olivia dropped onto the queen bed in her room at the Bourdens', exhausted after another day. She'd babysat for people before but only two weeks into nannying, and she wondered if she'd survive until the end of the summer. The kids were good, as long as she had something to occupy their interest. She'd learned quickly that Seth needed something to look forward to or a breakdown derailed their entire afternoon.

A familiar ringing pinged through the silence of the air, and she picked up the phone to see her sister trying to do a video chat.

"Hey Scar. What are you doing out this late?" Her sister's face was dark, and it sounded and looked like she was walking through the dark.

"Just heading over to a club with Greg." The way Scarlett emphasized the doctor's name made Olivia want to vomit. "I hadn't heard from you and figured now would be a good time to catch up."

Looking at the clock, Olivia made a face. "At quarter to

midnight on a Friday? Kids are in bed, and I watched a movie tonight. That's as exciting as I get these days."

Scarlett's voice dropped to a whisper, and the camera moved so Olivia could see her whole face clearly. "I think he might propose."

Bolting to a sitting position, Olivia said, "Who?"

"Greg. He keeps telling me there's something he wants to talk to me about. We're going to dinner tomorrow night, and I think it might be the night."

"What are you going to say if he asks?" Olivia's stomach tied itself in knots, a mixture of jealousy and surprise taking over her emotions.

Scarlett shook her head as if not believing what she'd just heard. "I'm going to say yes, of course."

"You love him? After two months of dating?"

"Three. We've been dating for three months, Liv." Scarlett's eyebrows shifted together, a deep line forming above them.

Olivia rolled her eyes. "Just don't get too excited. I don't want you to get hurt."

"You're such a downer. Just because you aren't dating anyone right now, you have to rain on my happiness." Scarlett growled and started walking again, the camera shaking.

"How's Mom?" Olivia's voice sounded shakier than she'd meant it to, but with the news from the doctor the last time she'd been there, it was possible more changes could have happened just as fast.

Scarlett's features softened, and she said, "She's good, I guess. Not much change so far."

"I've got a free day Sunday, so I'm going to come visit."

"Sounds good." Scarlett glanced away and grinned, nodding at something someone off camera said. "Okay, I've got to go. Greg is waiting at the door for me."

"Hey Scar?"

Her sister's face looked at the camera again. "Yeah?"

"Good luck," Olivia said, giving her sister a quick smile. "I hope all your dreams come true."

A pleased look slid over Scarlett's face, and she said, "Thanks, Liv. You too."

The screen went black, and every thought and emotion that could, played within Olivia, causing her exhaustion only minutes ago to turn into a second wind of energy.

A text came through and as she opened it, an excitement filled her.

I'll be on the first ferry tomorrow. Get ready to have some fun. D. :)

Turning on the TV mounted to the wall in front of her, she leaned back, knowing she wouldn't get to sleep at a normal hour now. Not after news like that.

* * *

THE PREVIOUS SATURDAY had been somewhat flexible with hours, as Mr. Bourden came to Nantucket for the weekend. Olivia had helped get the kids ready for the day, and the family had left for a trip together. A similar setup happened again, and she now understood why normal mothers often needed some time to themselves after a bajillion questions throughout the week.

Mrs. Bourden spent time with them here and there, but for the most part, she was out getting a manicure or going to lunch with friends, meaning the brunt of those inquisitive minds landed with Olivia. More than once, she'd had to pull out her phone and look it up, showing the kids the answers, even though they weren't reading complete sentences yet.

Occasionally, Olivia would peek out the windows, her

insides charged with excitement that Dawson would be there soon. Was he excited to see her too? Or was his text because she was like family to him?

She needed to get rid of the schoolgirl crush, but the harder she tried not to think about him, the more he would pop into her mind. It didn't help that she'd talked to Ruby the other day, reminding her of the relationship Ruby and Carson had again. What Olivia wouldn't give for someone to be there for her, especially in the rough spots.

She'd been through so many things by herself, and she knew she was stronger for it. But sometimes she wished her knight in shining armor would appear and help her conquer more than she did on her own.

Finally, a few minutes after three, she saw the SUV pull into the Holt driveway. She checked her phone every so often but still heard nothing from Ella, which was odd. The two of them had been together most of the time when Olivia wasn't working, whether it was at the Holt home or in town over the past two weeks.

Olivia pulled a book from the wall of shelves in the Bourden family room, picking one she'd wanted to read for some time. Tucking herself up onto the couch, she skimmed the first page, checking her phone every few lines.

What is wrong with me? Have I turned into some stalker high school girl who didn't get invited over for a party?

She knew Ella wouldn't ever do that, but part of her just wanted to know what they were doing over there. As she read, she felt her eyelids get heavy and soon enough, she was asleep.

The doorbell rang, and she jerked awake, unsure of where she was or what she was supposed to be doing. Looking at the clock, she saw it was almost five o'clock. She hadn't taken a nap that long since her time in college. Those were the carefree days when all she had to worry about was the term paper her English professor set for the class.

Opening the door, she saw Ella, Dawson, and Tony standing on the doorstep. Blinking a few times to help rehydrate her dry eyes, she said, "Tony? What are you doing here? I thought you weren't coming back until sometime this week."

The guy flashed them a smile, revealing his white teeth against lightly tanned skin. "I figured I'd surprise my girl. I missed her." He already had his arm around Ella's shoulders and pulled her closer to his side. He leaned down and kissed the top of her head.

"Okay, so what are you all doing here?" She didn't want to presume too much, but they had to be there for some reason. She gave a nervous look in Dawson's direction, and he grinned back. At least she had the doorjamb to keep her upright.

Ella moved a piece of hair out of her line of sight and said, "We signed up for a dinner cruise around the harbor. Come with. We have to leave here in about thirty minutes to board."

You couldn't have told me this earlier? She reached up and felt her hair, something she should have thought of before opening the door.

"A dinner cruise?" Her nap-foggy brain had a hard time understanding it all. Dinner cruises were for a romantic date night and as much as she wanted to fulfill that fantasy with Dawson, she knew he was still off limits.

"Yeah, it'll be a lot of fun, Liv. You'll come, right?" Dawson asked, his eyes pleading with her. She didn't know if that's because he didn't want to be the third wheel or because he wanted her to be there.

"I guess. What are you all wearing?" She looked at their regular street clothes, hoping they said they weren't changing.

Ella and Tony looked to Dawson for the answer, and he looked flustered as he said, "I think it said something about business casual. I'll probably wear slacks."

"I'll wear my maxi skirt. Comfy but nicer looking than jeans." Ella winked at her, and Olivia mentally cheered that the girl didn't always have to dress up.

The three of them turned away and walked down the steps. Dawson paused and turned back. "We'll come get you in about thirty minutes. Will that work?" When she nodded, he winked at her. Did people faint from things like that? Or was that just one of the exaggerations from the movies? Either that or she would need a knee replacement soon as she kept locking them into place.

Throwing on a pair of black pants, Olivia picked out a bright blue shirt with a scalloped edge along the bottom. Using the curling iron to add a few more waves to her hair, she applied some mascara and eye shadow, finishing right as the doorbell rang. She grabbed the charm bracelet her father had given her from the dresser and slipped it on.

Stepping into her small black wedges, she then stumbled down to the door with a small purse. Opening it, Dawson stood in the doorway. The button-up shirt was tailored right to his upper body and with his hair spiked up in the front, she had to force her brain and her mouth to connect.

"You ready?" he asked, holding out his arm for her.

"I think so," she said, stepping out of the house and locking the door behind her. Sliding her arm through his, she took a long deep whiff of his cologne and wished she knew the scent. It smelled like the sea, only a pleasant smell, sans fish.

As they reached the car, he leaned in and whispered, "You look amazing." He opened the door and helped her into the backseat before he walked around the SUV and got in on the other side.

Ella and Tony sat up front, Ella practically bouncing in her seat. "I'm so excited! I hope we see something on this cruise."

Tony turned to the back with a smirk. "She's only wanted to do this for forever. So, if she talks our ears off about it, blame Dawson."

Holding his hands up, Dawson laughed. "Please, I was just trying to keep the favorite brother spot by checking something off on the bucket list before my sister becomes an old married lady."

"Jeremy holds the favorite brother spot because I don't have to play therapist."

Olivia sighed. "I've missed Jeremy. When is he coming to Nantucket?"

Dawson gave her a strange look before saying, "He flies back from California this week."

"He was like the younger brother I never had." Olivia folded her arms over her lap and focused on the road ahead as much as she could, even though every nerve ending sparked that Dawson was sitting next to her, on a kind of date.

Was this normal for people one was attracted to? Did a person's brain go on the fritz like this or was that just how teenagers reacted?

She was so focused on her senses, she didn't hear much of the conversation on the way to the harbor. As she slid out the door, Dawson asked, "Are you okay?"

"Yeah, why?" She placed her hand in his, trying not to dwell on the tingle in her fingers as he touched them.

"You didn't say much on the way here." He gave her a look that was more questioning than angry.

She smiled at him and shrugged. "I just—it's been a long week. I'm excited for this though. What made you think of it?"

He nodded his head in the direction of the couple ahead of them. "Pretty soon, she'll be living in Europe, and I won't have as many chances to do fun things like this with her. She's always talked about doing a cruise like this, but my parents always said it was a waste of money. Now that my mom is older, I think she sees the value in little adventures like this."

"Do you talk to your mom a lot?" Olivia pulled a strand of hair away from her eyes, holding it behind her ear as the wind continued to blow just enough to annoy.

"Not as much as I used to. Since she married Phil, they're always jet setting to somewhere. But I'm glad she has someone. She was pretty lonely there for a few years." He gave Olivia a thin-lipped smile.

"I can imagine how hard that would be."

More than I care to admit.

"I haven't seen that charm bracelet in forever. You still have the charm Ella and I got you for your birthday."

Ella heard that and stopped to see. "Which one? I can't remember."

"The crab. We had just gone fishing and somehow Olivia caught a crab."

Tony's face crinkled, and he opened his mouth, ready to contradict them. Olivia held up her hand and said, "It wasn't a regular-sized one. It was a stray hermit crab. One of the boys in the neighborhood thought it would be funny and slipped it on the line when I turned away."

"I've never seen Liv scream so loud in my life." Ella laughed, and Liv felt the same embarrassment she had after finding out what Timmy Simmons had done. She'd almost forgotten the Holt siblings had given her the charm. How had he remembered something so small from so long ago? It made her wonder what other things he remembered about their time together. And the way he looked at her made her wonder if his feelings had moved past the sisterly stage. She'd just have to wait and see how things played out.

CHAPTER 16

*D*awson's feelings seemed to be out of whack that evening. Once she'd opened the door, he'd been blown away by Olivia's beauty, not masked by layers of makeup. He'd worried when she'd said something about Jeremy, wondering if she silently held a torch for him. But the way she interacted with Dawson, he didn't think that could be true.

Not that it should matter. This was supposed to be a fun adventure with the four of them before his sister's wedding. So what if his life wasn't all planned out yet? He'd figure it out sooner or later.

They reached the dock and checked in for the cruise, stepping on deck.

"This is absolutely amazing. I can't believe we're actually doing this." Watching his younger sister bounce with glee, he chuckled, glad he could do something as small as this for her. It had hit him, like really hit home on the ferry over earlier that day, that in a matter of weeks, she would be Mrs. Anthony Spencer and would move across the ocean to begin her new life. As happy as he was that she'd found someone like Tony, it still hurt to think that she wouldn't be there to laugh with him about something lame, or even to tease.

The women excused themselves to go to the restroom, leaving Dawson and Tony to lean on the bars and look out into the fading sunlight.

"How's work going, Tony?"

His future brother-in-law grinned and nodded. "Going pretty well. We've increased in several sales departments. And I'm going to tell Ella that we'll be moving to Paris after the honeymoon." The man was all smiles, and Dawson slapped him on the back.

"When she hears that, this dinner cruise will be a waste of time." They both laughed at that, knowing how much Ella had always dreamed of living in France. "So, the cosmetic line is taking off, huh?"

"Yeah, as weird as that sounds. What guy wants to say that he works in cosmetics?" Tony shrugged. "But honestly, it's good money and a needed industry."

"Will Ella work for you when you head over there?"

Tony made a face. "To be honest, I haven't talked to her about that. I'm already taking her away from her family as it is, I didn't want to pressure her into leaving work with you. If she wants to, there will be a job open for her. If she wants to do both, I'll support her completely."

"You're a good man, Tony. I couldn't ask for a better guy to marry my little sister. Anyone less would make it hard to be excited for the wedding."

With a hard slap to Dawson's back, making him wince, Tony asked, "What about you? Ella said you broke up with that one Garrett girl, right?"

"Yes." Dawson grinned. "At least she told you I broke up with her. She keeps trying to tell me I didn't make it final."

Tony motioned to where the women had disappeared. "So, what about Liv? Any possibilities there?"

A quick rollercoaster of emotions took off in Dawson's stomach. "I'm not sure yet. I mean, would that be weird to date my little sister's best friend?"

"People do it all the time. And if she's good for you, why not?" Tony's smile went even wider as he looked over Dawson's shoulder.

"Sorry, hopefully we didn't make you wait too long," Liv said, smiling at them.

One of the crew on deck approached, asking for names. He guided them to a table along the railing, and the four of them sat, enjoying the scenery.

"What did we miss?" Ella asked, looking between both guys.

Dawson looked at Tony, curious if he would spill the news now. Sitting back, Tony grinned and said, "I have some news I want to share with you." He looked around, as though he were trying to decide the best place for it. "Let's go over here and watch the dolphins while we talk."

Worry pulled at the corners of Ella's eyes, and Dawson couldn't wait to see what it looked like in a few minutes.

Olivia turned to him and whispered, "What is that about?"

Dawson smirked. "They're moving to Paris instead of England after the honeymoon. His company is moving its headquarters there."

A loud gasp came out of Liv's mouth, and she covered it with her hand. "Oh my goodness! She's going to die a happy woman." She licked her lips and smiled in the direction of Ella and Tony, but Dawson found himself studying her face. When she turned back to look at him, she asked, "What?" her eyebrows stitching together.

"How are you always so happy and content?"

She let out a loud laugh at that. "I have plenty of rough days, that's for sure."

Flustered, he leaned closer to her. "I'm sorry, I didn't mean to make light of your problems. I know they must be hard to deal with day in and day out, but you always seem to be moving forward." He wasn't sure if his sister could hold up as well as Liv had under the same circumstances.

"You're good. It's nice to think that's what you think though. Sometimes it takes a lot more work than I have energy for to get through the day."

A waiter brought a carafe of water and filled the glasses in front of them. Waiting until he moved away, Dawson tried to lighten the mood by saying, "How have your first two weeks of work gone?"

Olivia pretended to faint, lifting her arm over her face and dropping back against the chair. After a few seconds, she straightened up and smiled. "It's exhausting, but I really like it. Seth is the mischievous one, and I feel like I have to dangle a carrot in front of him or something to keep him busy; otherwise he's like a tornado through the place."

Dawson laughed. "Sounds a lot like Jeremy as a kid."

"I could argue that you were the same, from what I remember. You were always causing some sort of mischief and usually pulling us all into it."

With a straight face, he said, "I have no idea what you're talking about."

"Building a boat to cross the pond. You made Jeremy try it out first, and your dad had to run to fish him out before he drowned."

Dawson opened his mouth to defend himself but closed it when he saw the determination on her face. "Okay, so that plan backfired. What kind of activities have you done with them?"

"Picnics, trips to the park. We even visited the whaling museum this last week. Seth was bored within five minutes, but Rebecca stopped sucking her thumb long enough to walk through the building."

"I'm guessing that's a good thing?" Dawson asked. He didn't remember his parents having to worry about thumb sucking with the three of them.

"I'd say it's a huge step. They're good kids, they just need a little more face-to-face time with their parents, you know?"

Dawson felt his heart skip a beat as she looked at him. Without thinking, he said, "What would you do if you were their parent?"

Liv sat back and stared out across the water, her jaw working as she thought about it. "Honestly? I don't think I'd have a nanny."

"Really? Your future husband makes a ton of money, but you wouldn't have a nanny?" He watched the bright redness creep up her neck and into her cheeks, her gaze turning to the floor.

"We had a nanny sometimes growing up, but my parents would still do stuff with us quite a lot, especially my mother. Who better to learn from than someone who loves you unconditionally and isn't getting paid to do so?"

Dawson was blown away by her answer. She must have been mulling the conversation over in her mind because she said, "Okay, that sounded harsh. I mean that would be what I want. I know there are plenty of moms out there who are even better parents because of their time away at work or whatever occupies their time. I just think you have to find a balance for that, you know?"

Ella and Tony came over at that moment, ending the conversation as dinner was served at the same time.

"Paris?" Olivia asked.

"Yes! Can you believe it? I can't. I've already pinched myself several times. I never would've thought I'd be living in Paris!" Ella turned and hugged Tony again, pulling back just enough for a quick peck on the lips. Once she sat, she opened the napkin from the table and smoothed it over her legs. "You better come visit me."

Dawson saw Olivia shift in her seat under his sister's intense gaze. He didn't know everything about what she was going through, but he could imagine that nothing had turned out as she'd planned. He'd never heard her complain about her situation but after looking up moderate dementia in Alzheimer's patients, he knew the treatment was pricey.

"I'll do what I can." She smiled at Ella, but it didn't reach her eyes.

Something tugged at Dawson, as if attaching a cord between Liv and himself. His feelings about her were growing, and not just as the older brother of her best friend kind of way.

CHAPTER 17

Olivia had loved every moment of the dinner cruise. She'd fallen asleep on the way home and woke up to find Dawson carrying her to the door. It had been hard to keep her emotions in check at that point, and the temptation to bridge the few inches to his lips had been almost unbearable. She'd wiggled enough to get down before he walked into the house with her in his arms. That seemed a little too intimate.

He'd texted and came to find her every so often since then, which always brought a smile to her face. And the kids got excited when he was around.

Wednesday morning, as Olivia had just taken the kids outside to play, Ella called.

"I messed up."

Olivia's thoughts immediately turned to Tony, and she hoped nothing had happened to him or their relationship. "What's wrong?"

"I wrote down my fitting appointment for next week, but it's today. Can you come with me?"

"I have the kids all day." Olivia's mind took off, trying to think of options. "Maybe if I promise the kids an adventure out, we can come with."

"Good. Because I really need you to try on your dress too."

Olivia gulped harder than she should have, causing her to cough loudly. When she'd agreed to be Ella's maid of honor, she'd subconsciously known she'd have to wear a dress, but she hadn't put much thought into it over the course of the past few weeks. As much as she loved her friend, sometimes her color choices weren't what Olivia would have chosen.

"My dress?"

"Yes. I've got it all picked out. You'll look amazing."

Hesitating, Olivia finally said, "What are your wedding colors again?"

Exasperated, Ella said, "Sage green and rose."

Not the worst colors in the world. Let's just hope the fit of the dress isn't horrible.

"What time do we need to leave?" Olivia thought about the kids' schedule and what she needed to pack to keep them occupied and not starving.

"In twenty minutes. It's downtown and since it's lunch time, I'm worried about traffic." Ella was usually relaxed and fun, but when she was stressed, even the little things got to her.

Olivia said, "The lunch rush isn't as bad as Boston traffic, so we should be okay. I'll get the kids ready to go."

Hanging up the phone, she searched her mind for ideas of places that could be a reward for the kids' good behavior, but nothing came to mind. By the time Ella pulled up in the SUV, Olivia had convinced them with a vague special surprise that she hoped she could deliver on.

Getting into the backseat with the kids, Olivia jumped when she saw Dawson in the front passenger seat.

"Are you coming to the dress shop with us?" she asked, trying not to look too amused.

"Yeah, I didn't have anything going on, so I thought I'd tag along. Maybe I can hang out with the kids if you need me to." He waved to the twins and grinned at her.

Seriously, was he for real? There had to be something wrong with him, but she hadn't been able to figure that out yet, other than the fact he was dating another girl.

Yep, that was the kicker. Of course he was already taken. But she couldn't do a whole lot to keep her heart from falling in love, and part of her was ready for the consequences of it.

"Where's Tony?"

"He can't come see the dress, silly. Besides, he has a crazy amount of work to get done today and a couple of conference calls, he said. So, this will be a fun trip, and he won't feel guilty for not joining us."

Ella babbled the whole way, while Olivia opened the large bag she'd packed for the occasion. She gave Rebecca and Seth each a small package of goldfish crackers.

"Where are we going if we're good?" Seth asked, giving Olivia a cockeyed grin.

"You'll just have to be surprised after we get done with the dress shop." Panicking, she grimaced at Dawson, who grinned.

"What if we take you fishing after? Do you like fishing?" Dawson asked, looking between the two kids.

Seth and Rebecca both bounced in their seats. "Really? You'll take us fishing? I've always wanted to fish," Seth said, more excitement from him than Olivia had seen all summer.

"Well, if Liv says it's okay, then we'll take you out later today. We've got a bunch of fishing poles in our garage." Dawson wiggled his eyebrows, and the kids squealed with laughter.

Rebecca pulled her thumb out of her mouth to say, "Why

do you call her Liv when her name is Olivia?" It was such a small thing, but she was surprised Rebecca had noticed the difference.

"Ella and I grew up with her, and we've just always called her Liv. She's been a good friend to us, so it's our nickname for her."

Turning to look at Olivia, Rebecca said, "So, since you've been with us for a while, will you call me Becca?"

Olivia wrapped an arm around the girl's shoulders and pulled her in. "If that's what you want to be called, that's what I will call you."

They made it to the small dress shop down main street, and Olivia was surprised she was so nervous. Was it because Dawson was so close? Or was it just the fact a dress meant a wedding, which equaled her best friend moving to a foreign country?

The five of them walked into the shop, and a woman came from behind the counter, dressed in a well-tailored business suit. Her hair was a mixture of grays and whites, but she either had a fantastic hairdresser or a lot of good genes to get it looking like that.

"Good afternoon. Miss Holt?" The woman looked right at Ella, who nodded. Turning, the woman looked at the rest of them, a stern look passing over her face as she looked at the twins. "And who have you brought with you?"

"My brother Dawson, my maid of honor Olivia, and the Bourden twins." Ella pointed to each one in turn, and Olivia almost laughed as the woman's face changed to glee when she heard Bourden.

"My daughter is friends with Mrs. Bourden. It's so nice to meet you both." The kids looked to the ground and tried to turn away.

"Come on, you two. She said hello. All you need to do is say it back." Olivia bent down to their level, and they looked at her as though she was asking them to cut off their right arm. Finally, after a little more coaxing, they both waved and gave a half-smile.

The woman relaxed and smiled at Olivia, as if to give her a doggy treat for performing some incredible act.

"Let's move you over here. Miss Holt, we'll have you try on your dress first, and then I'll pull the dress for Miss Justice, is it?"

"Yes."

The woman removed her glasses and studied Olivia's face for several seconds. Olivia wasn't sure what to do about it, whether she should stare back or pretend to be helping the kids.

"Are you Peggy Justice's daughter?"

Snapping her head up to look at the woman, Olivia nodded. "I am."

In a sudden movement, the woman Olivia had thought prickly at first glance strode forward and hugged her. "It's so good to meet you. Your mother is an amazing woman. She helped me through a rough time in my life. Tell her hello from Rosie, will you?"

Olivia felt Dawson's hand on the small of her back, giving her the littlest sense of comfort. Forcing a smile, she said, "I will. Thank you."

Ella moved off with the woman, and Olivia's shoulders sagged as she felt the exhaustion creep through her back.

"Head back there with Ella. I'll make sure to keep the kids occupied." Dawson's words were soft as he leaned only a few inches away from her. He took her hand, and she squeezed it.

"Thank you." *For more than you know.*

CHAPTER 18

When Ella stepped into her gown, Olivia couldn't help but tear up. The top was a sweetheart neckline with straps over her shoulders, the bodice fitting her frame well. Around the waist, the dress flared out, the silk and tulle pieces making her look like a princess.

"Ella, you look amazing!"

"Do you think so?" Ella turned her nose up, one of her tells that she felt insecure.

"Are you kidding? You look like you should be on the cover of a bridal magazine. When did you pick it out?" Olivia waited for Ella's answer as Rosie pulled out several pins and tugged at sections of fabric along the sides of the dress.

With a smile, Ella said, "When my mom was here last. I think you were on the show at the time. I was worried I wouldn't find a dress at all here on Nantucket, but this was the third dress I tried on, and I loved it."

"What did your mom say about it?"

"You know my mom. She kept pushing other dresses at me the whole time, but she finally gave in by the end of the appointment." Ella laughed, but it didn't have a lot of humor in it.

Rosie turned. "It wasn't Mrs. Holt's first choice. Sorry, Mrs. Vandersleuven."

Ella waved her off. "She's still Mrs. Holt to me." Turning to Olivia, she said, "You know how my mother can get. She had a picture in her head of how everything would look, but I don't want the wedding to be so big that I don't know most of the people. I get that she knows a lot of people after being the head of the family business for a long time, but those people don't want to come to a wedding. I want it to be a bunch of friends celebrating our nuptials."

"Did you tell her all that?" Olivia asked, biting the inside of her cheek. Mrs. Holt had always been an opinionated woman, but she hoped the woman could see what her daughter wanted and go with it.

With a nod, Ella said, "I did. It took a few days for her to cool off, but I think she'll be fine. She's not coming back from Europe until a few days before the wedding, so I don't know if that's her permission to do what I want or her stubbornness to get her way."

"Stay strong, Ells. I know how she can be sometimes, but it's your day to celebrate, not hers."

Ella set her jaw and said, "That's right. It's my day. It should go how I want it to go."

Rosie stood up and said, "Okay, I think I've got it all pinned. Let's take the dress off slowly, and we'll get it fixed up. I'll need you to come in one more time, probably two or three weeks before the big day just to make any last-minute tweaks."

The woman whisked the dress away as Ella got dressed. Before Olivia had a chance to start another conversation, the woman had returned with a dress bag. "This is the dress you picked out, Miss Holt."

Ella walked over and looked inside, nodding and smiling at Olivia. Rosie laid the bag on the bench and unzipped it all the way, revealing an odd green-colored dress. Trying to school her expression, she smiled and nodded.

"It looks, um, great."

Rosie held it up and motioned for Olivia to prepare to try it on. With a few tugs, they zipped up the back of the dress, and she wanted to laugh at her reflection in the mirror. Even Rosie tried to keep her expression neutral.

"What do you think?" Ella asked, her voice unsure.

"You're the bride. What do you think?" Olivia said, hoping to not have to say what she really felt.

Ella grimaced. "It looks awful. Not that you aren't beautiful, but you look like a…"

"Giant avocado?" Olivia said, unable to hold in the laughter for another minute.

"Yes!" Ella said, near crying at this point. Even Rosie shook with laughter.

Striking a few poses, Olivia asked, "Do I still have to wear it?" She made a crazy smile, showing all her teeth.

Shaking her head, Ella said, "No. I love you too much to make you wear something you hate." Turning to Rosie, she asked, "Do you mind if we look for something in the store?"

"We should probably check on Dawson. Do you think he'll be okay?" Olivia worried he would be bugged since the kids were her responsibility.

Ella disappeared for a moment and came back in. "He said he's good. He's going to take the kids down the block to get an ice cream."

"Really?"

With a big smile, Ella said, "Dawson loves kids. Hopefully, it doesn't take him too long to start having them. He'll be a great father."

Olivia felt warmth flood her body, and she was surprised

steam wasn't coming from her cheeks. What was with her insides turning on her like that? Ella hadn't even pointed out Olivia as being a candidate.

But the thought of Dawson hanging out with little mini-Dawsons made her heart melt.

Thinking of his hand on her back earlier only made her wish things could be like they were in her dreams.

CHAPTER 19

"What do you two like to do?" Dawson asked the twins as they sat in the ice cream shop down the way. He'd treated them to double scoops and from the wideness of their eyes, he wondered if they'd ever had anything so big.

Seth licked his chocolate scoop and said, "We like to do a lot of the stuff Olivia does with us. She helps us get our homework done really fast, and then we go outside and do fun stuff."

Dawson took a lick from his mint chip cone and nodded. "You have homework in the summer?" He'd gone to a private school growing up, but he'd never had homework before he'd even entered kindergarten, at least from what he could remember.

"Yeah. Mom says it's good for us," Rebecca said, a slight lisp sounding through.

They seemed to be good kids, and it was heartwarming to hear that they liked Olivia. Dawson's phone rang, and he looked down to see his brother's name.

"Jeremy, how's it going?"

"Hey, bro. It's going well, except I think someone forgot to come pick me up. Are you at the house?"

Dawson felt the dread that came with forgetting something, and he said, "No, we're down Main Street. I'll come get you quick. Are you at the harbor?"

"Yeah. I'll just hang out here for a minute. I've got too much stuff to walk that way."

Hanging up, he looked at the kids and said, "Okay, we're going to take this ice cream to go. Grab a few napkins in case we spill."

"Where are we going?" Seth asked, licking at a drip on his hand.

"To pick up my younger brother. He's just over at the ferry."

"Did you forget about him?"

Dawson made a face and said, "Yeah, I forgot he was coming to the island today. Are you ready to meet him?"

"Is he fun?" Rebecca asked.

"Not as fun as I am," Dawson said, winking at them, "but he's good at making people laugh."

They loaded up in the SUV, and Dawson texted Olivia where they were heading so she didn't worry about the kids.

It took just a few minutes to make it through town with all the traffic. As they pulled into the parking lot by the ferry, Dawson saw Jeremy sitting on his luggage next to the curb. Pulling up alongside him, Dawson got out and gave his brother a hug.

"How was the flight?" he asked, taking one of the suitcases to the back of the vehicle.

"Not bad. It was the ferry that killed me today. You'd think I'd be used to the sea after all these years." Jeremy stood about a head shorter than Dawson, and his face looked more like their mother's.

The two of them slipped into the car, and Jeremy saw the kids in back. "Whose kids are these?"

"The Bourdens. Liv is nannying for them this summer."

"Liv Justice? She's back on the island?" Jeremy's face split into a grin, and a small cut of jealousy echoed through Dawson's chest.

"Yeah, she's staying with them." He gave his brother an eye, as if to clue him into the fact that she was living in the place she'd called her summer home for years. Jeremy nodded, and Dawson put the car into drive.

"Is Scarlett here with her?" The change in Jeremy's voice made him wonder which of the Justice sisters his brother was fonder of.

Shaking his head, Dawson said, "No. She's back in the city. I'm not sure what she's doing. Liv never said anything."

With one eyebrow raised, Jeremy asked, "So, what are you doing with the kids?"

Laughing, Dawson looked back to see the twins listening intently, still licking at the now smaller cones.

"Ella forgot she set up her fitting today, and Liv needed to go along so she could try on her dress. I think Ella wanted her to see the wedding dress because she's still a little hurt about Mom's comments."

Jeremy leaned his arm against the window and rested his head in his hand. "Poor girl. It would be easier if she just realized she needs to do her own thing and let Mom be mad about it for a moment."

"Yeah, but it's her wedding. She was hoping Mom would come around by now, you know."

They pulled up next to the dress shop, and Dawson parked. "I'll run in and see if they're ready. If not, we can go do something around here."

He jumped out of the car and walked to the door of the

shop, pushing it open. The bell rang, and Rosie's voice called out, "Be with you in a minute."

Looking around, he wasn't sure what to do. Striding forward, he stood next to the curtain.

"I'm just wondering how much longer you'll be here. Jeremy just got in."

Ella's face appeared at the side of the curtain. "Jeremy? Oh no! I forgot about him coming today."

With a wave, Dawson said, "It's all right. We picked him up. We just wanted to know if we should go do something for a while longer or if you're ready to get some food."

Stepping out from behind the curtain, Ella said, "Liv is just changing back into her clothes."

"How's the dress?" He tried to stay neutral, like he didn't care, but he was curious about how she would look in a more formal gown.

"The first option didn't work out, but we found something better."

Rosie pulled the curtain open, and Liv stepped out with a smile, slinging her purse over her shoulder.

"Let's get some food. I'm sure the kids are hungry." She smiled at him before walking toward the door of the shop.

Scratching his neck, Dawson made a face. "Well, I, uh, treated them to two scoops of ice cream. So, they might not be ready for real food soon."

Rolling her eyes, Liv said, "Way to go, spoiling their lunch." She hit him with the back of her hand on his chest and laughed.

Heading out to the car, Jeremy stepped out and hugged Ella and then Liv. He pulled back long enough to ask, "Where's Scarlett?"

Had he not heard Dawson's response to that question earlier?

"Who knows? I was expecting to hear that she was

engaged, but she hasn't called me. I should probably check on her though."

By the innocent expression on Jeremy's face, Scarlett was the one he was curious about, maybe even pining for. Who would have thought he and his brother would like the Justice sisters?

CHAPTER 20

The Bourdens took the twins on a trip for the weekend and since it was an event with Mrs. Bourden's family, Olivia wasn't needed. Having three days to do as she pleased after nearly three weeks of constantly going with the kids, she wasn't quite sure what to do with herself.

She'd made a trip into Boston to see her mother early, hoping to catch her mother on a good day. Her mother slept for a good portion of the time Olivia was at the care center and when she did wake, she was in the same frame of mind as the last time Olivia had been there, calling her Livvy and talking about dolls. Dr. Turner explained that all the recent tests they'd given Peggy Justice hadn't shown much difference from before, giving Olivia a sliver of hope that things would level out for the foreseeable future.

Olivia headed back on an afternoon ferry, her emotions moving like an airplane in turbulence. The stress of her mother's health and how Olivia would be able to pay all the bills once this summer ended weighed heavily on her. At least with the paychecks she received every two weeks, she was able to save money, enough to get the Justice women through at least Thanksgiving. If only Scarlett would get a job to help, it would ease some of the panic building inside her.

Her phone rang, and Olivia smiled when she saw Ella's name.

"Hey, girl!" Ella said. "What are you up to?"

"I'm on the ferry on my way back to Nantucket. You?" Olivia leaned against the rail, staring out at the island. Nantucket had always been her happy place, but she wasn't feeling super ecstatic. It was like her life was stuck in limbo, not able to enjoy the things of the past but also fretting for the future.

"Come over. We'll do something fun. I need a break from finalizing wedding plans."

Olivia agreed and after dropping off the Bourdens' SUV they let her use, she walked over to the Holt house, a small duffel bag in hand. Ella let her in and sent her upstairs to put her things in the room she'd stayed in a few weeks earlier. As she sat in the silence of the room, she again wondered what she was doing with her life. This nannying gig was great, better than she'd even hoped but with only five weeks left of summer, a familiar pit formed in her stomach. She'd need to figure out the next step before she left Nantucket.

Pushing the anxiety aside, she lay on the bed and breathed in and out slowly, calming her mind.

A knock came at the door, and Olivia didn't move. "Come in."

"Oh, are you all right?" Instead of the feminine voice of Ella, she was surprised by the Dawson's deep baritone, causing her to sit up. She brushed a strand of hair behind one ear and tried to figure out what to do with her hands.

"Fine, thanks. Just tired." She smiled at him, pulling her knees up and hugging them to her chest. He returned the smile, the silence settling over them as they stared at one another. Finally, Olivia asked, "Did you need something?"

Dawson almost jumped, as if he'd been in a trance. "Oh, uh, yeah. We're getting ready to watch a movie out in the theater. Ella asked me to check on you while she popped some popcorn."

Olivia stood. "I'll be right down. I think I'll change into some sweats."

His lips curled up, and his eyes twinkled with amusement. "That's a great idea. I like being comfortable when watching a movie. Wait for me." He grinned and closed the door behind him.

What was she going to do about him? Why did he have to be so cute all the time?

Okay, Olivia. Focus. He's dating someone else, might even be engaged. Her heart echoed back that it didn't matter, she was at the cliff, and there was no turning back. Heartbreak Avenue straight ahead.

Pulling on a pair of llama pajama pants, Olivia threw on a t-shirt and waited by the stairs.

"I can't believe you beat me," Dawson said, running his hand through his hair as he walked toward her.

"It's a skill," she said, laughing. They descended the stairs to the main floor and turned to another set leading downstairs. "What are we watching?"

Dawson turned to her, his expression thoughtful. "That's a good question. It's probably not my turn to pick anyway."

Olivia couldn't help but laugh. "Wait, you two are still taking turns? You're how old again?"

"Eleven." He chuckled, the deepness of it rumbling through Olivia. "No, it's been awhile since we've watched a movie together. I always just assume it's her turn."

"I'd say that's a smart move on your part." Olivia grinned at him before stepping into the theater room.

It was exactly how she remembered it. The large tiered couches were a light-brown leather that turned into recliners. The dark red on the walls with the dim light made the room dark, but it was perfect for watching a movie projected onto the other wall.

"Ella is bringing the popcorn," Dawson said, stopping at the door. "I forgot about drinks. Any requests?"

"Water."

Dawson smirked at her. "Why am I not surprised? Still a camel, huh?"

Olivia laughed. "Yep. Are you still a Coke addict?"

"Maybe," he said, his smile more mischievous than before. He turned and disappeared around the corner.

Olivia walked up to the back row, settling into a spot near the middle. Sinking into the softness, she closed her eyes, relaxing in the silence. With so much commotion the past week, the silence was peaceful, even though a part of her missed the twins.

Ella came in with a large bowl of popcorn, some smaller bowls in one hand. She moved to the back row and settled into the recliner next to Olivia, setting the large popcorn bowl in the space between them. Handing Olivia a small cereal bowl, she said, "Take what you want."

As they both lifted the leg rests, Ella pulled a blanket from the shelf next to her, tossing one to Olivia before covering her own legs with one.

"Wow, you guys still know how to watch a movie," Olivia said, throwing a few kernels of popcorn into her mouth.

"Comfort is necessary. What do you want to watch, girl?" Ella raised her eyebrows to Olivia and pointed to the shelves at the other side of the room. Rows and rows of movies lined the shelves, and Olivia had to squint to see some of the titles.

It had been so long since she'd had time to watch a movie.

With a devilish smile, she said, "How about a chick flick? Do you still make Dawson watch them with you?"

Ella frowned. "Oh, please. He's had to live with me for all but three years of his life. It was always a trade off with the rom-coms and the action/adventure movies." Dropping her voice a little, she confided, "I've been training Tony for a while now. Sometimes he even asks me questions about the movie."

The two girls laughed, chewing on the kernels of corn. Ella stood and walked over to the shelves. "I think I know which one you'll want to watch, Liv." She pulled a case down but obscured the cover and title, making Olivia curious.

Dawson walked in with a few drinks in his hand, Tony on his heels with napkins. Depositing a can of root beer next to Ella, Dawson handed Olivia a bottle of water before dropping down next to her. The scent of ocean and musk swept over to her, and she tried to inhale without showing she was melting at the scent of him.

"Thanks for the water," she said, focusing on the bottle cap as if it would explode if she took her gaze from it. She hadn't been this close to a guy in a long time. And since that guy was Dawson, she had a hard time knowing how to react.

"No problem. What are we watching?" His gaze drifted to Ella, who was inserting the disk into the system in the wall.

Olivia shrugged. "She said it would be a surprise."

Moving the popcorn bucket, Tony sat next to where Ella had been a few moments before. "Am I trying to be supportive tonight?" He laughed when Ella shot him a dirty look.

"Yes, this movie is a classic, and I expect you to take notes. I'll be giving you a pop quiz after." She winked at her fiancé, and Olivia didn't realize she'd sighed until she saw Dawson's head turn in her direction.

"Everything okay?" he asked, with a hint of a smile on his lips.

Olivia closed her eyes and laughed, squeaking out, "I'm good."

When he was only a few inches from her ear, he whispered, "Is it okay if I sit here?"

With her insides screaming, Olivia nodded, unsure of what her mouth might say if she let it open at all. All her teenage dreams were being fulfilled, and her heart was celebrating. He'd always sat over a few seats when they'd watched movies in here before. Was he sitting this close because he wanted to? Or because this felt almost like a date with the two lovebirds next to them? A thought came to her, and she turned to him, suddenly serious.

"Aren't you dating someone?" The words were a little louder than a whisper, but she was surprised she'd had the nerve to even say anything. That question was like a laser beam highlighting her own feelings, and she wasn't ready to be that vulnerable.

His half-smile and shake of the head made her stomach flip, even as she tried to keep her face neutral.

"We broke up last week."

Biting her bottom lip, Olivia said, "I'm sorry. Are you okay?"

His full smile broke through then, and he said, "More than okay."

"Where's Jeremy?" Tony asked.

Ella shook her head. "He said he had a migraine. We'll have to do something with him tomorrow."

The movie started, and Olivia gasped. "The Shop Around the Corner? I haven't seen this since the last time I was here."

"I figured. It was always your favorite movie." Ella smiled and walked back to her seat, tucking the blanket around herself and Tony.

"What's this show?" Tony asked in a loud whisper.

Ella nodded. "Remember *You've Got Mail*?" When Tony nodded hesitantly, she said, "This is the older version of it with Jimmy Stewart. It's fantastic."

"Dad's favorite." The words were nothing more than a whisper on Dawson's lips, his jaw clenched and his eyes glossy.

Without thinking, Olivia reached over and touched the back of his hand, trying to convey that she understood. He gave her a sad smile and slipped her hand into his, holding it gently.

As every alarm went off in her head, she worked to reassure herself that he probably just needed some support. She still missed her own father after four years. She couldn't imagine how he felt after eight.

The show began, and Olivia let herself sink into the fairy-tale created on the screen, of two unlikely people falling in love. She could let herself dream about it for a few more minutes. Let reality hit in the morning.

CHAPTER 21

As much as Dawson tried to hide the tears while he watched the movie, several drops escaped down the sides of his cheeks. He could remember all the times his father had held him on his lap while watching Miss Novak realize she loved her pen pal and coworker. As tough of a businessman as he'd been, Scott Holt had been a romantic at heart.

At one point, Olivia left for a moment, claiming she needed to use the bathroom. He'd felt the absence of her warmth next to him, especially in his hand, where the electric jolts had been almost constant. She'd come back only a minute or two later, carrying several tissues. Handing him one, she proceeded to wipe under her own eyes.

He could only nod a thank you, the tightness in his throat making it difficult to swallow, let alone speak. Dabbing at the tears, he blew his nose as the movie came to a close, memories flowing through him. The credits scrolled across the screen, and he leaned over to see both Ella and Tony asleep.

"Thank you for this," he said, holding up the tissue.

"No problem. I usually keep them around when I watch

movies, but I forgot to grab some before it started. I tend to cry at the littlest things." She gave him a small smile, grateful her expression was without pity. It had been a long time since his father passed, but their relationship had been something he'd never forget. Scott Holt had worked quite a bit throughout the years, but he tried to make up for it when he was home. In these little moments, Dawson wondered what life would be like if his father were still alive.

"I can't believe those two fell asleep. Do you want to watch something else?" He heard the hopefulness in his voice and tried to keep his expression neutral. How did he all of a sudden have feelings growing like a wildfire for someone he'd known for almost two decades?

Olivia pulled her hand up and looked at the watch on her wrist. "Wow, it's still early. I think I could handle that."

"What do you feel like watching?" He turned to the wall of movies and squinted, trying to read some of the titles. Now that she had settled into the blanket again, he didn't want to move.

She turned her head, trying to see as well. Shaking her head, she leaned back against the recliner, turning her bright blue eyes toward him and said, "I'm too tired to get up and look." Her laugh hit home in his chest, creating a feeling he didn't know he could feel. After the laughter died down, she asked, "What is something you've always wanted to do? Like, bucket list type thing."

The question surprised him. Looking up at the dark ceiling, he searched his brain for the answer. Growing up as a Holt, the number of things he'd been able to do was probably more than most. "I don't know, to be honest. There are so many things I've been able to do already. We've gone traveling a lot as a family, and I've been able to do a lot of the daring things, like jump out of a plane."

"I still can't believe you did that. I think I would die of

fright in the plane right before I had to jump." Olivia's eyes went wide as she gave him a look.

"What about you? What have you always wanted to do?" He turned enough that he could stare at her profile, admiring her long lashes and round-tipped nose.

Blowing out a breath, she said, "I would love to travel more. Even just a road trip across the country. Get to see how people live, see if things really are bigger in Texas." She paused, her eyes narrowing in on the black screen in front of them. Only the faint glow from the wall sconces allowed him to see her expression. "We traveled a lot when I was younger, but that was to a lot of cities. I'd love to do more camping, hiking, and see some of the national parks."

Dawson chuckled at that, his mind still turning as he sought for what he really wanted. "Do you go many places now?"

Olivia shook her head and breathed deep. "It was hard when my father died because we were so close as a family. Then Mom's diagnosis made it so we had to sell the Nantucket house and our house in Belmont. It's been eye-opening to see how much we had. I've been so focused on helping my mom, I haven't really thought about any trips."

"But you went on *The Suitor?*" Dawson grinned. He'd been curious about it once he'd seen her on the last episode. He wanted to know exactly what had convinced her to do that.

Holding out her hands, Olivia sighed. Pink tinged her cheeks, and she squirmed, more uncomfortable than he'd ever seen her. "Well, Ella gave me a gift card to a match-making place for my birthday—"

"Love, Austen?" Dawson said, louder than he intended, and the couple next to them stirred. After they settled down again, he turned to Olivia, waiting for her to continue.

"Yes. How did you know?" Her surprise made him smile.

"She gave me one about six months ago, hoping I'd break

up with Adelyn at the time. I took those personality tests and everything just to make her happy, but haven't followed up with the program." Olivia gave him a close-lipped smile, and he felt like pop rocks were going off in his stomach.

She bit her bottom lip, and Dawson waited. "So, I went in and did the tests, like you said. A week later, the owner called me in to say I was one of the matches for a guy who was going to be on the reality show." Twisting the tissue around her finger, she continued.

"At this point, with the pressure to help my family, I hadn't really been dating or anything. And with everything going on with my mom, I think I kind of needed an out for a bit. So I told myself that if I made it to the end of the show, it would be like winning the lottery or something. And, if I could find someone to love and who would love me, even better. It was a risk and in the process, I lost my job at the salon, but I also got to come back here, enjoy a place that holds so many great memories for me."

When she paused, he realized she wouldn't say much more. "What did you think of Carson? Not the heartbreaker everyone always painted him to be, huh?"

"You know him?" Her mouth dropped open, and Dawson stared at her pink lips for a few seconds too long.

Nodding, he said, "I get together with a group of guys on Saturday mornings. We row down the Charles River, and I met him there. We all had a good laugh when he told us the proposal made by his agent to clean up his image." Narrowing his eyes, he asked, "Did you have feelings for him?"

Olivia smiled, her eyelids growing heavy. "On those shows, they make you feel like you should be feeling something for the guy, but it just didn't stick. When I found out Ruby's history, I was kind of rooting for her, you know?" She yawned, covering her mouth with the back of her hand.

Feeling the panic ebb, Dawson looked down at their intertwined fingers. It was such a simple thing, but he wanted to sit there, holding her hand forever. When he glanced up, he saw her eyes closed, her lips parted.

It was then he realized what he wanted to do most. He wanted to marry his best friend, to have someone at his side who would understand the ups and downs, encourage him through whatever came his way.

Would that mean marrying Olivia? She was a better candidate for all that than most girls. And from the way his feelings soared each time she was around, he was way past the liking stage.

CHAPTER 22

The next day was quiet at the Holt home, and Olivia wasn't sure what to do. Being a Friday, Tony, Ella, and Dawson all had several meetings and things to get done for work, leaving Olivia with an open day. Jeremy had come down with the flu and had sequestered himself in his room. Olivia made sure to check on him every once in a while, hoping to make him feel a little bit better with enough fluids to keep him from being dehydrated.

She took some time to walk on the beach and spent most of the afternoon curled up with the book she'd never finished from the day they'd gone on the dinner cruise.

At several times, she found herself staring out the window, thinking about the evening before. It had been near perfect, with Dawson right next to her, talking and laughing. The holding her hand part was even better than she could have pictured it, and she felt like she should have been born in the Regency era for all the gushing she was doing over a simple touch.

She'd wanted to kiss him, especially after he'd told her he'd broken up with his girlfriend. But she'd held back, for what reason she wasn't quite sure. It could've been that the last time she'd kissed him had been like a fairytale, standing next to the lighthouse at sunset, until the next day when her world had come crumbling down around her. Part of her worried that something similar could happen again, and she didn't know if she could survive the heartache one more time.

Did he even remember that kiss? Or was it just some fling to him, like he'd kissed so many other girls he couldn't remember? Not that he was a player, but just that he'd had a lot more girlfriends than she'd had boyfriends. The thought of the last question made her chest hurt, and she pushed all the thoughts of kissing Dawson away, hoping to save herself before the real damage was done.

She'd tried calling Scarlett again, but the phone kept going to voicemail. It wasn't uncommon to have radio silence from her sister, but Olivia had expected some news after the last phone call they'd had. Would she already be engaged to the doctor? A small seed of jealousy grew in her stomach, and she did her best to push it away. If her sister were really engaged, she'd be happy for her. She'd just have to remember that things didn't always work out right when she wanted them to, but the little miracles usually followed.

Before dinner, all the working people emerged from their makeshift offices, and Ella proposed a bike ride. It had been years since Olivia had ridden a bike and while it took awhile to get comfortable again, she had to admit it was fun. As they rode back up the driveway, the sun had begun to set, making for a beautiful backdrop.

Exhausted from the long ride, she dressed in her pajamas once she got back to the house, this time sporting pants with flying pigs on them. She felt like a kid who'd just spent all day at an amusement park, with all the adventures she'd had in the month since she'd come to Nantucket.

After trying to sleep for over an hour, she got up and walked downstairs to the kitchen. Opening several cupboards, she found the mugs and a box of hot chocolate packets. They weren't her favorite, but they'd have to do to help her sleep.

She placed the mug filled with milk and the contents of the chocolate packet in the microwave. As the seconds ticked down, she stood back and leaned against the counter, chewing on a fingernail. Her mind replayed the race down a long stretch of road with Dawson during the ride. The smile on his face in the memory left her weak in the knees. Goodness gracious, he had a great smile. That boy would probably haunt her dreams after this trip, and she hoped it wouldn't leave a permanent ache in her chest.

"Hey! You couldn't sleep either?" Dawson asked, causing her to jump.

"No. I'm tired, but my brain won't shut off." The microwave beeped, and she held the mug by the handle as she pulled it out. Steam rose from the liquid, and she blew a couple of times before taking a small sip.

Dawson pulled down a mug of his own and moved to fill it with water. He popped it in the microwave and stood across from her.

"Wait, you don't mix yours up before you put it in there?" Olivia asked, pointing to the microwave.

His eyebrows raised high, and he said, "No. You do?"

"Yes. I can't believe you use water for yours. Milk is the only way to go."

The corners of his mouth turned up, and he shook his head. "You milk people are crazy."

"I guess it could be worse. You could be a person who only drinks hot chocolate in winter." She tried not to grin as she moved to the counter and sat on a stool, blowing on the hot chocolate to keep her insides from going on the fritz.

Once Dawson's hot chocolate was done, he pulled it out and mixed in the packet, the sound of the spoon hitting the sides echoing in the quiet room.

"I'm going out on the patio. Do you want to join me?" He raised his eyebrows, the corner of his mouth turning up.

What could a little time outside hurt? She was already falling for him. This was just a summer to remember, at least that's what she was telling herself.

Olivia nodded, and they took seats on the deck chairs facing the pond in the backyard. The sky was near black, with hints of dark blue streaked throughout. The sound of the lake lapping against the beach twenty yards away was soothing, and Olivia leaned back into the chair, curling her legs up underneath her.

"This is perfect." It was a whisper, but she saw Dawson's head nod in agreement.

"Sometimes it's nice to have a quiet place to reflect after the day."

After a sip of her hot chocolate, she looked at his profile, enjoying the strong set of his jaw. Breathing in the air, it seemed as though some of her worries were slipping away for the moment, making it easier to relax.

"Are you checking me out?"

Olivia had just taken another sip, and it came shooting out of her mouth as she tried to hold in a laugh. "No, but I'm so sorry," she said, wiping his sleeve with her hand. Hello, muscles.

"You're fine," he said, laughing. He sobered after a minute and said, "Do you ever wonder why life takes some people from our lives and leaves others we'd rather not have there?"

Standing up halfway, Olivia said, "Well, I can go inside if that's how you feel." Part of her did it out of humor.

Reaching up, his hand wrapped around her wrist, and he said, "No, I don't mean you. Please stay." When she'd settled back in, he said, "I could hang out with you forever. I just mean, some people can only be managed in small doses."

"You've got that right. Scarlett being one of them. I love her, I just need a break every once in a while from her excessive enthusiasm."

Dawson grinned and said, "Excessive enthusiasm. A nice way to say they won't give you a minute's peace."

"Or things are amazing one minute, and the world is ending the next. She called to say she might be getting engaged to the doctor who oversees my mother. But that was over a week ago, and I haven't been able to get a hold of her since. Sometimes it's nice to step away from the rollercoaster and take a relaxed kiddy ride." She bit the inside of her cheek as she shook her head, realizing how much it was true.

"Adelyn, my ex-girlfriend, has been texting non-stop for the last eight hours."

"Oh?" Olivia couldn't help her curiosity seeping through. She held her breath, hoping to find out Dawson's real feelings about Adelyn and herself. Couples got back together often enough after a breakup. She just hoped he wouldn't reconsider.

He ran a hand through his hair and sipped from his cup. Olivia wondered if he would ever answer, when he said, "I guess it's strange when you think you want something, until you take a step back and examine it from a different angle. Or something changes your perception."

"Do you have mixed feelings about proposing to her?" The words poured from her lips, but she needed to know, needed that confirmation that she wouldn't just be a rebound chick, if their relationship progressed further.

"I didn't at first, but looking back now, there were warning signs I just missed. I thought we were the same, that we had a lot of the same goals. But when she kept trying to string me along, not giving me a direct answer of yes or no, I just got tired of it. As much as girls gush over proposals in movies, it would be nice to show the guy's perspective for just a minute. He's putting a lot out there, in the hopes that he's loved in return."

"I've never really thought about it like that, but you're right. I guess that's what we're all hoping for in life, to love and be loved in return." Olivia smiled at him before turning her gaze to the stars.

A silence fell over them for a few moments until Dawson asked, "Have you heard anything about your mom?"

"I visited this week, but nothing has changed."

He reached over and covered her hand with his, warmth pulsating through her hand and her chest. "I'm so sorry, Liv. I should have kept in touch better over the years."

The tenderness in his voice caused tears to prick at her, her eyes filling with moisture. "It's not your fault. I haven't even told Ella all of it. My mom doesn't remember me anymore, just talks to me like I'm her older sister, and they're still living at home, or like I'm still a child. It breaks my heart to see her like that, especially since it came on so quickly." She wiped at the tears flowing down her face, staring into the darkness to avoid looking at him. Why did she have to cry in front of him?

The back of his hand brushed against her cheek, wiping at the tears on that side. She wanted to lean into his touch, but she sat still, enjoying the moment. He pulled her toward him, letting her lean her head against his broad shoulder. "I'm here. I'll always be here to listen when you need it."

It was the sound of a promise she didn't think he could keep, not in the way she would've liked. Her head slid a little, and she could hear his heartbeat drumming along. He smelled of a fresh breeze and chocolate. She breathed in deeply, hoping to capture this moment for the lonely moments in the future. She lifted her head as she thought about it, locking her eyes with his.

He leaned in an inch, and she did the same, her breathing hitching as her heart thundered off, as if starting a race. He closed the rest of the distance, his lips connecting with hers lightly. Every nerve ending fired, sending shockwaves throughout her body. She wouldn't be surprised if fireworks had gone off behind them.

The door squeaked open, and Olivia jerked back, eyes wide. She bit her upper lip and smiled at Dawson, who did the same to her before turning to see Jeremy in the doorway.

"Am I interrupting anything?" The mischievous look told her he'd seen the kiss, and heat traveled up her neck and into her cheeks.

Yes. Just the best moment of my life.

CHAPTER 23

*D*awson had no problems going to sleep that night, his dreams filled with the recurring kiss with Liv. He could've kicked Jeremy to the curb for interrupting their moment together.

Running a hand through his hair the next morning, he could still feel the softness of her lips on his. And his body had reacted as though he'd forgotten what it was like to kiss a girl, even though it hadn't been that long ago. Their first kiss four years ago was top three on the list of kisses he'd had, but the one last night took the top spot without question.

He dressed, pulling on a pair of khaki shorts and a maroon tee, a goofy smile on his face the entire time. Walking out to the kitchen, he found Ella and Tony sitting at the bar, eating cereal. Olivia stood at the stove, spatula in hand as she flipped some eggs.

"Morning, sleepyhead," Ella said, seeing him standing there. "It's nice of you to grace us with your presence."

"Oh, please. It's barely eight in the morning. It's not like you're in a hurry to go anywhere." Ella made a face, and Dawson laughed at her.

"How did everyone sleep?" he asked, sweeping his eyes over the engaged couple and focusing on Olivia. A hint of a smile crossed her face as she slid the eggs onto a plate.

"Good. Do you want some eggs?" She looked at him, giving nothing else away in her features.

The smell of the eggs was tantalizing. "I can make them. But thank you." He grinned at her again, feeling a jump of electricity between them, even at five feet apart.

He pulled two eggs from the carton next to the stove and cracked them into the warm pan Olivia had just used. With a little salt and pepper, he scrambled them until they were mostly dry, sliding them onto a plate. After cooking some toast, he spread butter over both pieces and took them back to the bar, where he set them next to Olivia.

Sliding his chair closer to her, their arms touched as they ate, neither one pulling away. They gave each other a smile here and there but tried to pretend they were listening to Ella drone on and on about everything that still needed to be done before the wedding. Was this really all women could talk about months and weeks before their wedding?

Jeremy walked in, noting the proximity of Olivia and Dawson, a hint of a smile on his face before turning to the fridge.

"How are you feeling this morning, Jeremy?" Olivia asked, her tone sincere.

"Much better, thank you. I think I'll survive whatever we've got planned today." He pulled out some juice, drinking straight from the carton.

"Put juice on the list. I'm not drinking out of that box anymore." Ella's disgusted voice made Dawson laugh louder than he should have, and everyone turned in his direction.

"What's up with you? You've been acting strange since you walked into the kitchen."

Raising a hand, Dawson reined in the laughter and said, "Never better, sis."

"Have you heard from Scarlett?" Jeremy asked, after sending a knowing smile in Dawson's direction.

"No. Have you?" Olivia asked, stabbing a piece of egg with her fork. "I've tried calling and texting several times, but I haven't heard anything. She's done this before but has usually contacted me by now." She ate the piece of egg, chewing it slowly.

He turned away, not answering her question as he popped some bread into the toaster. What interest did Jeremy have in Scarlett? Dawson flipped through several memories when the two families were together, holidays and birthdays, but everything with Jeremy and Scarlett together was usually clouded with the reminder of time spent with Olivia. He'd have to corner his brother later into telling him.

When Jeremy turned around, he directed his attention to Ella and asked, "What are we planning to do today?"

"Let's hang out here, play in the water, lay out." Ella's words caused Tony to turn from the newspaper they were sharing.

"You don't want to go anywhere? I feel like we've been inside the house forever since yesterday was so long with work and all."

She shrugged. "As long as it's low key, I'm game."

Jeremy's phone buzzed, and he looked down, his face relaxing and a smile covering it. When he glanced up, he said, "I've got to take the car really quick. I'll be back in a few."

Without waiting for questions, he turned toward the garage door, grabbed the keys from the hook, and disappeared.

"What was that about?" Olivia wondered aloud.

"I'm not quite sure," Dawson asked. "What is it *you* want to do today?"

He knew Olivia often deferred to what others wanted to do, trying to be agreeable.

"I actually like Ella's idea of hanging out here. What about you?" She raised her eyebrows as she took a bite of her toast.

"Let's do it. After breakfast, swimsuits and hanging out back."

Ella laughed. "Why, thank you. We can go out for dinner or something so Tony doesn't go stir crazy."

Dawson watched as Olivia grinned at that. She moved her arm, and it bumped into him. She looked down and moved her arm a few more times, smiling as she hit him. When she stopped, she left her arm next to his, causing an almost electric sensation to creep up his arm. He glanced at her lips and realized how much he wanted to return to their interrupted kiss from the night before. Maybe he could find a way to get her alone later in the day.

The rush of feelings every time he glanced her direction now was something he'd never had while dating Adelyn. And the more he thought about it, those feelings had all started back with that last day of summer on Nantucket four years ago. He'd forgotten about it as his and Olivia's paths had gone in different directions for a while, but he didn't want to forget this time. Dawson wanted to remember every glance, every smile, every electrically charged moment.

He just hoped she felt the same.

CHAPTER 24

They'd retrieved every sand tool they could find in the basement of the house and moved to the beach, laying out towels and putting up a couple of umbrellas.

Olivia wore a striped light-blue one-piece, the straps tying around her neck. She'd seen Dawson come out of the house carrying a few of the fold-up beach chairs and had to turn around so he didn't see her cherry-red face. He looked amazing in what looked like Hawaiian flowers, the colors blue, red, and white. His upper body was model worthy, and she had to fight to keep the smile off her face.

With everything set up and it only being nine-thirty, Olivia was excited to spend the day outside, reliving much of the memories she held of the island. Setting up one of the chairs under an umbrella, she sank down into it, enjoying the easiness of the scene. She'd missed this.

A chair squeaked as it opened next to her, and she turned to see Dawson grinning down at her. "Is this spot taken?"

"By you, of course." She waved as if she were being gracious and then leaned back in her chair.

Another chair squeak sounded on her other side, and Ella slumped down, setting her sunglasses on her nose as she leaned back, her breathing slow and steady.

Smiling, Tony stood before them and said, "What happened to wanting to play in the water?"

"Maybe later," Ella said, her voice soft and relaxed. "This is perfect for now."

Tony moved off, wading through the pond. Olivia closed her eyes, wishing this summer could last forever and that her problems could all just disappear. But then again, the changes to her life from her father's death had led to meeting some extraordinary people.

She wasn't sure if she'd fallen asleep, but a familiar voice pulled her out of the relaxation stage of the day.

"You all look so cute out here in your beach chairs," came a voice behind her.

Standing, Olivia turned, shading her eyes from the sun so she could make sure it really was her younger sister. With her heart beating and cheeks hot with embarrassment, she moved over to the deck, where her sister stood.

Trying to be calm, she asked, "What are you doing here, Scar? I've been calling you for days, and now you just show up here?"

Jeremy walked out the door and stood next to her at the railing. "Jeremy came and got me from the ferry." Scarlett slid her arm through Jeremy's and leaned her head on his shoulder.

"That's why you didn't say anything when I asked if you'd heard from her." She narrowed her eyes at Jeremy, and he dropped his gaze to the deck, fighting a smile. Turning to her sister, she said, "You've been contacting him but not your sister. Thanks a lot, Scar."

"Oh, don't be sad, Livvy. I lost my phone and only got a new one yesterday. I have Jeremy's memorized from when we were kids, so I figured I'd see if he were around." The twinkle in Scarlett's eyes said she was only sharing part of the truth.

Looking over at Jeremy, Olivia said, "Can we have a few moments?" When he finally looked up and realized she was talking to him, he nodded.

Turning to Scarlett, he said, "I'll get my suit on. See you out there in a few?" He raised an eyebrow, and Scarlett nodded. When he disappeared, Olivia pulled her sister into the living area just inside the back door.

Leaning toward her sister, Olivia asked, "What happened to the doctor?"

The mask of happiness fell from Scarlett's face for a few moments before the cheery expression returned, although this time it seemed forced. Tears formed, and the little red splotches that always showed up when she cried, turned her face into a red and white mess.

"What's going on, Scar? You've been even more odd than usual."

"Love you too, sis." She took a minute, staring at her fingernails before she moved to the couch and flopped down on it. The tears slid down the sides of her cheeks, and Olivia wished she could somehow take whatever pain she felt. "Turns out that instead of proposing, Greg wanted to tell me that he'd been dating another girl at the same time and had just proposed to her." When she looked up and caught Olivia's gaze, Olivia's heart broke just a little bit for her sister.

Reaching out, she gathered Scarlett up into a hug, not sure she could give any real advice that would soothe the pain. She tipped up her sister's chin to look at her.

"Are you all right? Why didn't you call me about it?" She searched the girl's green eyes, wishing she could pull all the secrets out through them so she could protect her sister from things like this.

Sobbing, Scarlett said, "Because I didn't want you to be worried about another thing. And, since I usually screw up my relationships, I was hoping to stave off the humiliation longer."

"So, you did what instead?"

Giving a half-smile, Scarlett said, "Wallowed at home. It's a disaster." She lifted her hands and said, "Don't worry. I'll have it cleaned before you come back."

Tucking a stray piece of hair behind Scarlett's ear, Olivia repeated, "Why didn't you call me? I would've come for you."

"I didn't want to jeopardize your job." Looking around, Scarlett seemed to put the situation together. "I thought you were a nanny at our old house."

"I am. The kids are gone with their parents until tomorrow night. I saw Mom the other day and was thinking of going again tomorrow. Have you gone to see her?" Olivia reached forward and took her sister's hand.

Scarlett nodded. "I went a couple of days ago. She didn't recognize me at all. I thought she might be coming back at one point, when she talked about Nantucket, but there wasn't much to connect us anymore."

Thinking about that, Olivia asked, "What's going on with you and Jeremy? You seem pretty close all of a sudden."

With a coy smile, Scarlett said, "He comforted me after a few of my broken relationships, so I called him on a whim. Turns out, he's really good at listening."

"Are you hoping for a rebound relationship or do you actually like him?" Olivia was surprised by her tone. For some reason, she suddenly felt defensive of the Holt family, even with her own sister around.

Leaning back, looking appalled, Scarlett said, "I can't

believe you said that. I've always liked Jeremy, even when he didn't look like he does now. Just another bonus, I guess."

"Just be nice and don't hurt anyone." A surge of acid crept up her throat, and she swallowed, trying to clear it away. She knew she should probably be on the side of her sister, but at this point, she didn't know where they stood. Scarlett obviously didn't trust her to not fly off the handle or point out that she'd warned Scarlett to be careful about the doctor.

"I'll try, sis. It might be hard, but I can figure it out."

"Where are you planning on staying?" Olivia asked, irked that she didn't know all the plans of her sister's trip.

"Here. Jeremy said I could stay in the guest bedroom upstairs."

Another pit of jealousy boiled over inside Olivia, and she nodded, trying to keep her thoughts to herself. She'd be working with the kids all week while Scarlett got to hang out and do whatever she pleased in the meantime. They needed to figure out a better, fairer situation for the two of them. Because Olivia couldn't support her sister forever.

CHAPTER 25

As much as Olivia had tried to convince Scarlett to come with her to visit their mother, Scarlett refused, using the excuse that she didn't want to see Greg again. She couldn't blame her for that though and took off on the earliest ferry to the city the next morning.

By the time she arrived at the Jones Center, it was close to nine in the morning. She wandered outside for a few more minutes, knowing official visitor hours didn't begin until then.

When the time came, Olivia walked through the sliding glass doors at the front and checked in. She retraced the steps she had taken several times before and ended up in an empty room with the bed made. No visible traces of personal belongings sat along the windowsill or on the small table in the corner. Olivia's heart beat as if she'd been running a marathon. Had she been worrying too much about a boy and her mother had suffered to the end alone? No, the nurses would have called her with any new developments.

Running to the nurse's station, she tried to compose herself before saying, "Where is Peggy Justice?"

The nurse looked up at her and smiled. "Are you a relative?"

Olivia resisted the urge to reach out and hit the woman. "I'm her oldest daughter."

"Let me see. Olivia?" When Olivia nodded, the woman said, "Yes, she's been moved to room 212. But right now, it looks like she's in the rec room. Just go down this hall and take a right. The doors will be a ways down on the left."

Slapping the counter with her hand, Olivia said, "Thank you," before moving off in the direction the woman pointed.

The adrenaline eased up, and she told herself to breathe now that she didn't have that guilt riding over her. Walking through the door, she stopped and glanced around, trying to locate her mother. After one quick sweep, she had to slow down and look over each of the patients placed around the room.

Finding her mom over in the corner, Olivia took long strides, stopping when she was just a few inches in front of the wheelchair. The beautiful long, brown hair, the thing her mother prided herself in, had been cut to her shoulders, several grays running through it now. Her face looked as though it had aged several years in a matter of weeks.

Kneeling down, Olivia tried to put that out of her mind as she said, "Hi, Mom. It's me, Olivia."

"Olivia?" Her mother raised her head and blinked a few times before she recognized a face in front of her. "You look just like my little girl. Have you seen her? She was playing over here just a few seconds ago." Moving her eyes, her mother searched for what Olivia assumed was her at a younger age.

Taking her mother's hands in hers, Olivia whispered, "Oh, Mom. I've messed up everything. I need to just focus on finding a job and taking care of you. I don't know if I'll ever find a guy who can be direct about his feelings and not be lame." After the appearance of Scarlett at the Holts', Olivia had made an excuse as to why she needed to head back to the Bourdens. She'd waited like a sappy girl to hear from Dawson, but a text or call never came.

A wide smile crossed her mother's features. "Lame boys can sometimes be the best of the bunch. When I met my David, it was love at first sight, but it took him awhile to get the picture."

"So, what did you do?" Olivia hadn't heard much about how her parents had gotten together, just that once they did, not much could separate them.

"Well, he was dating another girl, and I just bided my time. They eventually broke up, and I, being the good friend and confidant, was able to be there for him. By that time, he finally realized he had feelings for me. Our first kiss was like a firework show." Her mother's beam suddenly turned somber, and she looked like a scared little child. "Who are you?"

"Olivia."

"I don't know you. Please leave me alone." Her mother scowled and turned her head away from Olivia.

Hesitating for a second, Olivia stood and backed away slowly, her mother's eyes watching her with every step. She'd lost so much already, and now she was losing her mother. The sweet memory and the softness of her mother's face gave Olivia a glimmer of hope. But then the sudden change and lack of recognition hurt as much as the day she'd lost her father. Holding back the tears until she got outside the care facility, she found a nearby bench and sat, the tears dumping like buckets. Why did it have to be so hard?

CHAPTER 26

With all the activities and the arrival of Scarlett the day before, Dawson barely had time to see Olivia. She'd left early that morning in a cab, and it took a minute for him to remember that she'd planned to visit her mother.

Fully awake a couple of hours later, a reminder sounded on his phone. Thank goodness for Barbara's ability to schedule reminders because he'd forgotten about the business trip he was supposed to take to Chicago that afternoon. Jumping in the shower, he washed faster than he had in a while, pulling on some dark slacks and a button-up shirt as he stuffed several clothes into a small suitcase. With his toiletries packed up, he knocked on Ella's door.

It took more than a minute for her to open it, but she looked at him through sleepy eyes. "What?"

"I forgot I have a flight to Chicago in four hours. Can you drop me off at the ferry?"

Rolling her eyes, Ella said, "Yeah. Just let me get changed."

Dawson hurried downstairs, checking the times the ferry departed. If they hurried, he'd be able to make the high-speed one, and then he could catch a cab to Logan Airport. Taking the T would make him late, and he didn't want to go through the hassle of rescheduling if he didn't have to.

Tapping his foot and checking his watch every ten seconds, Ella finally walked downstairs five minutes later, looking like she was sleep walking.

Grabbing the keys from the hook on the wall, he said, "I'll drive. I'd like to get to the dock in one piece."

She scrunched her nose and stuck her tongue out, not happy but too tired to put up a fight.

When they slid into the SUV, Dawson asked, "Why are you so tired?"

Ella opened one eye and looked at him. "I stayed up late going over the latest numbers and researching some new marketing techniques. I was so engrossed in it, I didn't realize it was four in the morning when I finally went to bed."

"New techniques, huh? What made you want to do that?" Dawson looked at her and then back at the road as he pulled out of the driveway.

She shrugged. "I just don't want us to lose any ground with sales. If there's something out there that can help the company, I'd better do my job and figure it out."

"Have you thought about what you'll do when you move to Paris?" He knew it probably wasn't the best time to ask his marketing director about her future but as her brother, he was curious.

"I've gone back and forth about it. Tony said I could stay with the company, or there would be a spot to work with his company. So, I think I'll figure that out after the wedding."

Dawson hoped it would be sooner, so he'd have time to train a new marketing person, should she decide to quit. He left her alone the rest of the drive, her lids struggling to stay open. He drove into the parking lot at the dock and put the car in park. Ella didn't move.

He leaned over and pushed her shoulder back and forth a couple of times. "Hey, we're here. I've got to run. Will you be okay to get back to the house?"

She laughed. "Of course, I'll be fine."

"Okay, well, blast the music if you have to. Just don't fall asleep on the way back." He hurried and pulled his suitcase out, waving as he jogged over to the ferry.

He heard his phone ring, but he didn't have a chance to catch it before the call ended. Once aboard, he looked down and saw a missed call from Liv. Pressing the call button, he heard the dial tone several times and wondered if she'd answer or if it would go to voicemail.

When the phone clicked, he heard a muffled sob. "Liv? Are you okay?"

"She was there, talking to me about how she and my dad met, and then all of a sudden, she acted like I was some stranger there to attack her."

Each of her sobs hit him in the chest, and he felt his lungs constricting at her pain.

With soft words, he whispered, "I'm so sorry, Liv. What are you feeling right now?" He cringed as he said it, the words sounding lame to his own ears.

"Frustration, sadness. Like every time I see her, I'm losing her all over again." She paused a moment. "Sorry, did I interrupt something? I thought about calling Ella, but I know she was up late."

"No, I'm glad you called. I just wish I were there to help you."

Silence sounded on the line until she finally said, "I've already lost one parent. How am I going to survive losing another?"

"She's not gone just yet, but when she is, we'll do it

together. Losing a parent is never easy, and we'll all help you, make sure you get through it."

She seemed to consider that because she said, "Thanks. Well, I've got to get back to the ferry. I need to get back for the twins this afternoon. What are you all doing today?"

Dawson frowned, wishing he could wait for her to come back and comfort her. "I have a business trip in Chicago, so I'm heading to Boston now. Do you want me to stay?" He couldn't delay this trip anymore; it was the last big push to cement a merger with one of the companies there. It was something they'd been working toward for the past two years, but if she asked him to, he'd make sure it got changed.

"Oh. No. Thank you for the offer though. How long will you be gone?" The curiosity in her voice caused his hope to lift.

"About a week. I'm hoping to get it done in the first two or three days, but this is a big business deal, which means they always run longer than I want them to." He hoped it would only be a week as he was already counting down the time until he could be back on Nantucket.

"Be safe. Text me pictures. It's been awhile since I've been there." She already sounded happier, and he hoped he'd helped, even just a little bit.

He smiled, even though she couldn't see him. "I will. You'll call or message me if you need anything, right? Even if it's just to vent about your sister, or my sister, I don't care."

She laughed then, and it pulled some of the tension in his chest free. He hoped she'd be okay. Before she said goodbye, he said, "When I get back, let's go to dinner, just the two of us." The words had streamed out and as scared as he was for her reaction, it was what he wanted. A chance to explore a relationship with her.

"That would be nice. Let me know when you'll be back."

He hung up, looking out over the land coming near. Stepping off the ferry, he looked around but didn't see her. She wasn't walking up the sidewalk to the ferry nor was she in line at the ticket booth. He got in a cab wishing he didn't have to go to Chicago right then. Wishing he could stop and help her feel better before he took off. This would be a long week without her.

CHAPTER 27

By the time Olivia made it back to Nantucket, she felt at least a little better. She wasn't sure what had made her call Dawson instead of Ella, but she was thankful she had. At least she'd had something to look forward to for the coming week. A dinner for just the two of them? She could consider that a date, right?

The week went fast at times and then at other times, the minutes passed like years. The twins learned a lot, and she'd taken them on a longer bike ride for one of the days. Most nights, when the kids were in bed, she'd go to the Holts' and watch a movie or play games until late, making her wonder why she tortured herself when the alarm went off every morning.

Occasionally, she'd get a text from Dawson, and she'd read and reread the words, analyzing them for anything significant. Even though she should be over it by now, she still hoped he'd take a certain interest in her. She'd know for sure after dinner that weekend, at least that's what she kept telling herself.

On Saturday, after getting the kids ready and sending

them off with their dad to head out on the family boat, Olivia made her way over to the Holts'. In a lot of ways, it felt like old times, how they'd gone back and forth between houses when they were kids.

As she walked in, she called out, but everything seemed oddly silent. She walked out the back door and saw a few people in the pool.

"Hey! How's the water?" she called out, and Ella turned, grinning at her.

"It feels awesome compared to the heat today. Grab your suit and join us."

Running back to the Bourdens', she changed as fast as she could and ran over in her flip flops and with her swim bag over one shoulder. She'd cut across the grass but saw movement near the front door of the Holt home and stopped to see if she recognized the woman. Walking a few steps closer, Olivia called out, "Everyone's out back."

The woman turned, pulling off her sunglasses. She had auburn hair and was several inches shorter than Olivia. Something about her seemed familiar, like she'd met her or seen her somewhere, but Olivia couldn't place it.

"Thank you." The woman smiled and walked out onto the grass, not stumbling even in her high heels. "Are you going that way?"

Olivia nodded and waited to walk beside her. "I nanny for the family who lives next door, but I've been good friends of the Holts for most of my life."

The woman pursed her lips and said, "I've known them for a couple of years. Some of them are very generous, but there are a couple in the family I could do without."

"Oh? I'm Olivia. What's your name?"

They'd rounded the corner of the house, and the whole backyard came into view. They were almost at the pool when the woman said, "Adelyn Garrett."

Olivia stopped walking, but she took advantage of leaning onto a beach chair so it wouldn't look like the identity of the woman had rocked her. Here was the girl Dawson had proposed to. What was she doing here?

Ella climbed out of the water and walked over, not recognizing Adelyn until she was a few steps away. "Olivia, who did you find?" She folded her arms over her chest and said in a curt tone, "Adelyn."

Adelyn's face held the same distaste, and she responded with, "Ella. Where's Dawson? I thought he'd been staying here the past few weeks, but he's not picking up his phone."

"He's on a business trip." Short and to the point. Olivia saw sparks in Ella's face and had to bite her lip to keep from laughing aloud.

She glanced down and dug through her bag. Finding the bottle of sunscreen, she opened the top of it, focusing on rubbing the cream on her arms so that Adelyn wouldn't see her expression. She knew Ella could get feisty at times, but to see her like this right now made the shock of meeting Dawson's girlfriend or ex-girlfriend a little better.

"I've been trying to contact him for the past week. I wasn't sure if he'd changed his number suddenly or not."

Laying on the sarcasm, Ella said, "I'm sure he's just been busy with this trip. It's a big deal for our company, so I'm sure he didn't want to get distracted."

Olivia smiled to herself, thinking about the handful of texts she'd received from him over the past few days. It made her feel good that he was at least thinking of her.

Adelyn frowned. "When will he be back?"

Tony came out of the pool and stood behind Ella. "In an hour or two, right, babe?"

Ella shot him daggers, as if she'd wanted to keep that a secret, but Tony didn't see it. "Yeah. He just texted that he was getting on the ferry."

Olivia's heart leapt at the thought. A small moment of doubt clouded that happiness as she turned on her phone to find no messages from him to her.

Taking a few steps, Adelyn moved in front of one of the beach chairs and took a seat, adjusting her sunglasses from her head to over her eyes. She raised her hand to shade her eyes, the sun glinting off something on her left hand.

"What are you wearing?" Ella moved forward, grabbing Adelyn's hand and inspecting the ring.

"The ring my fiancé gave me," she said, yanking her hand out of Ella's grip.

Stepping forward, Ella's face turned beet red, and she waved her finger at the woman before her. "You never said yes. There's no way he would have given you our grandmother's ring to keep if you never gave him an answer."

"You must not know him like I do then. I've already announced it to all my followers and the media. They should be reporting our engagement as we speak." She gave Ella a fake smile before saying, "I'll just wait for him if you don't mind. You there, would you mind taking my suitcase inside? It's out on the front porch." She'd pointed at Tony and while it took him a minute to register the words, he nodded and walked through the house to the front door.

Ella frowned, her jaw working back and forth for a minute before she dove back into the pool. Olivia hadn't been able to move, trying to reconcile the woman's words with everything Dawson had told her. Was she playing some angle?

When Olivia had finished applying her sunscreen, she jumped in the pool, trying to keep her thoughts from Dawson. She didn't know the entire story yet, and she didn't want to think he'd lied straight to her face. Since her emotions were so close to the surface, the pool was perfect for hiding whatever it was she couldn't control.

He'd be there soon enough to confirm or deny the story, and she didn't want to mope while she waited. When she broke the surface of the water, she saw Scarlett and Jeremy at the other end of the pool. The two of them were so close, almost cuddling in the water.

That was fast, Scar. From heartache to another guy in seven days or less. In her mind, it sounded like one of those gimmicky ads, and she laughed to herself at the thought.

The five of them soon forgot about Adelyn, playing water basketball with the hoop on the other end. Olivia wanted to forget that Dawson could walk through the door at any moment, but she kept checking, trying to make it inconspicuous. Scarlett swam to her side and whispered, "He'll be here soon. You're leagues above that girl. I hope he picks you."

And just like that, she was transported back to *The Suitor*, feeling the anxiety and nerves she'd felt every time there was a flower ceremony. She didn't want to have to compete for Dawson if it meant manipulating people. Ruby hadn't done that, but she had history with Carson to aid her there.

Sure, she and Dawson had summers of history, but would that stack up against the girl he'd dated for the past two years and to whom he'd proposed? Someone who hadn't gone through major life changes over the past four years.

As if knowing her brain was going into overload, she heard the door open, and Dawson appeared, looking rumpled but still attractive in his coral button-up shirt. He flashed them a smile and made eye contact, the grin deepening for her. Flutters and stings attacked her stomach.

"How's it going, everyone?"

The five of them in the pool waved, and Tony asked how his trip went. Before he could say much, Adelyn sauntered over and stood next to him. He turned, and something like fright appeared on his face.

"Adelyn. What are you doing here?"

"You didn't answer any of my texts or calls, so I thought I'd come find you."

"Why?" Olivia was surprised by his tone of voice on one word but finding her ex-boyfriend here would throw her off too.

Adelyn looked up at him, taking another step closer, her finger trailing up and down his forearm. Olivia glanced at the others in the pool, everyone riveted on the display happening before their eyes.

Moving onto tiptoes, Adleyn pulled Dawson down and kissed him. Olivia looked away and then back, hoping they'd be done at that point. He finally broke away, wiping his hand across his lips.

"Yes. My answer is yes."

Storming off, Dawson walked into the house and slammed the door behind him. Adelyn followed as fast as her heels would let her, and Olivia sank under the water, holding her breath until she was far enough under to scream. So much for a happily ever after.

CHAPTER 28

"Why did you come here? I told you before, it's over between us." Dawson could feel the anger boiling up in his chest, a volcano ready to erupt.

Adelyn smiled at him. "No, you said to take as much time as I needed to think about it and then see where you were when I'd made a decision. I want us to be together." She moved forward, trying to lace her fingers with his. He pulled away, taking a step back.

"You could have wanted that weeks ago. What changed your mind?"

"I was out with some friends the last few nights and realized how much I've missed being with you." Her expression felt off, more practiced than genuine, and Dawson looked away. "You aren't going to kiss me, baby?"

Putting up a hand to stop her progress toward him, he said, "No. We're not dating anymore, Adelyn. You didn't care enough about me to keep me around before. Don't think that a few words and a kiss will make things right that fast."

"What do you mean? I've missed you like crazy. Didn't

you get my messages?" She looked at him, sticking her bottom lip out more, trying to look innocent.

"I did." He clenched his teeth and watched as the expressions changed on her face. "I've been really busy with work."

Adelyn folded her arms, her lips pursed. "Well, after days of texts, the least you could do was send a message that you got them."

Shaking his head, Dawson threw out his arms. "No, you're not getting it. You're mad about a few days. Adelyn, I waited weeks to hear whether you wanted to marry me. And now you think you can just snap your fingers and get everything back that fast? I don't think so."

He stormed to the kitchen, needing a drink to help his mouth from feeling like a desert.

Pulling out a glass from the cabinet, he filled it to the brim with water and gulped, hoping it would help clear his thoughts. She stood near the counter, her lower lip trembling. This was the most somber he'd ever seen her, and he hoped she finally got the picture.

Her voice was quiet when she spoke, but the words were clear enough to understand. "Tell me what to do to fix it."

"It can't be fixed, Adelyn. We're different people. We just need to move on."

"I was out with a big group the other night, and James proposed to Tina at this club, and it was the cutest thing ever. When I saw how happy she was, I thought of us and how happy we could be together." Shaking her head, she walked toward him, wrapping her arms around his waist. "We have so much going for us. Give me a few days to prove it to you. If you still feel the same by the end, then I'm gone for good. But I do want to marry you."

Dawson didn't move as she kissed his cheek, his gaze locking with Liv's as she walked in from the back door.

Liv waved her hands around, and her mouth opened and

closed without a sound until she said, "Sorry, I was—I had to get something." She darted out of the room, and the expression on her face tore apart his insides.

"You've already missed the last ferry, so you can stay until tomorrow. But then I want you gone."

Adelyn pierced him with her gaze, her jaw set. "You've fallen for that girl, haven't you?" She motioned in the direction Liv had gone, and Dawson's eyes followed, hoping Liv would pop out, and everything would be okay.

"I fell for that girl long before I knew you. But I'm just now realizing it, and I don't want to mess it up. I appreciate the time we had together, but I think you could find someone better."

He pushed away from her and moved down the hall, his eyes darting back and forth in the hopes of finding Liv there. A search of the first and second floors came up empty, and when he walked back out to the pool, everyone was getting out, no Liv in sight.

"Looks like you messed up." Leave it to Ella to put things bluntly.

"I don't really feel like hearing the 'I told you so' speech right now, but if it will make you feel better, let's get on with it." He gave her a bored look and waited for the lecture to follow.

Ella sighed and then said, "Olivia went back to the Bourdens. What happened in there?"

He could negotiate deals and instruct several employees at Holt Packaging, but when it came to women and relationships, he wasn't sure which side was up. "Adelyn told me she wanted to marry me, and Liv walked in right then. She left, and I told Adelyn it wouldn't happen between us."

"And what's next?" Ella leaned forward on the counter, as if he would only reveal the secret by whispering.

"I have no idea. Maybe I should just head back to Boston

in the morning. Make things easier on everyone." He frowned at her and asked, "Why are you pushing so hard? What scheme do you have going on that involves my love life?"

"I think you have feelings for Liv. The sooner you cut ties with Adelyn, really cut ties, the better those chances are of you not screwing it up."

"Since when did you become so observant?"

"I've always been this way, you just didn't realize it." She patted his chest as she dried herself off with a towel. "So, what are you going to do about her?"

Taking in a deep breath, Dawson shrugged. "I don't know just yet. I know I have feelings for her, but does she feel the same? And if she does, would she believe me when I tell her that I'm not actually engaged to Adelyn?"

"Liv has liked you since we were ten. And seeing how she's looked at you over the past month, I'm sure it's not a crush anymore. As far as believing you about Adelyn, you'll just have to ask her and see."

Scrunching his nose, he asked, "Do you think I should go over there now?"

Swatting him with the back of her hand, Ella said, "Git. Otherwise, you might lose your chance."

CHAPTER 29

Olivia had run faster than she had in some time, making it through the gate in the fence and into the Bourden house in under a minute. She'd even rushed past Mrs. Bourden, who'd looked concerned and called after her as Olivia bounded up the stairs. But she couldn't stop, couldn't even breathe.

What had she done to deserve all the pain and the heartache? She wasn't sure she could take much more and once she made it to her room, she collapsed onto the bed. It was her own fault she'd let herself believe in the hope that things could work out, all while he had a girlfriend or an ex-girlfriend still hanging around.

Reflecting over the last hour, she wondered what Dawson could have been thinking in proposing to a girl like her. She seemed so opposite of everything he was about. And why was she still here if they had broken up? To reclaim him as her fiancée?

Or had they broken up? As she thought over the conversations she'd had with Ella and Dawson over the past week, she doubted whether what he'd said was true. And if he really hadn't broken up with her, the kiss she'd shared with Dawson… She couldn't think about it.

Curling into a ball, she sobbed until her head ached. She'd told herself she shouldn't get too close, shouldn't even dream that she could be with Dawson.

A knock came at the door. "Olivia?" Mrs. Bourden whispered.

Wiping under her eyes, she turned toward the door. "I'm so sorry, Mrs. Bourden. It's just been a rough day."

"It's Shaylee, remember?" She walked into the room, sitting on the corner of the bed. "And I'm not too old to understand. Why don't you tell me what happened?"

Gaining control of her sobs, she related the condensed version of her relationship with Dawson Holt, her voice cracking every so often as she thought about Adelyn hugging Dawson inside the Holt home.

Shaylee patted Olivia's leg. "Girl, this is when you decide if he's worth fighting for. What would your life be without him? I had to do the same for Will. He was dating another girl, and I just walked up and told him I liked him. A few days later, he'd broken up with the other girl, and we started dating." She gave Olivia a warm smile,

The bell rang downstairs, and Olivia stilled. "I can't face him right now. Not yet."

"I'll take care of it," Shaylee said, "Just don't take too long deciding. You'll feel better once you've at least told him how you feel."

Olivia could only nod, swallowing past the mound formed in her throat. She stood and walked to the door, holding her breath as she listened for the conversation at the door.

"Dawson, what brings you by?" Shaylee said. Olivia smiled. The woman was good at acting innocent.

"I'm here to see Olivia." His breath sounded rushed, like

he'd run over here too. Part of her wanted to leap downstairs and see what he had to say, what explanation he'd give for what she'd seen in the kitchen. At least it hadn't been a mini makeout session that time. Her skin still crawled as she pictured Adelyn's lips all over Dawson's.

Olivia held a breath as she waited for Mrs. Bourden's answer.

"I don't think she's up for visitors right now. She said something about feeling sick and needing to lie down. I'll tell her you stopped by though, Dawson."

"But, if you'll just—"

"Give her some time. I'm sure in a day or two, she'll be fine."

Thank you, Shaylee.

She was right. Olivia did need time. Time away from him so that her heart could heal, or at least put itself back together piece by piece. She thought of Shaylee's words to tell him how she felt, but how could she do that if he would always have Adelyn trailing him?

As she thought about all the people she'd lost over the years, she realized she was the common denominator. She couldn't control her father's passing, but it seemed like every time she got close to getting something she wanted, it got yanked out from underneath her. And she wasn't sure how much more of that she could take.

About ten minutes later, the bell rang once again, and Olivia prayed it wasn't Dawson again. When she heard Shaylee say hello, she knew the woman didn't recognize the person.

"Hi, you must be Mrs. Bourden. I'm Scarlett, Olivia's sister. Can I see her for a moment?"

"As long as you don't force her to leave, I think that will be okay."

Olivia listened as they climbed the stairs and then took

the few steps to her door. With a light knock, Shaylee called out, "Olivia? Are you up for a visitor?"

Wiping at the tears, she said, "Yeah, let her come in."

Scarlett walked in, her face somber. She slid onto the bed behind Olivia and raked her hands through her long hair. "Are you all right, sis?"

"No, but I'm glad you're here."

"Ella volunteered when Dawson came back, but I told her I'd come."

Olivia reached up and grabbed Scarlett's hand, squeezing it. "Thank you. It means so much to me that you're here. I just wish I had been there for you after the Greg fiasco."

Scarlett waved it off. "Honestly, you didn't miss much. I think on the heartbreak scale, it was only a two and a half out of five." She grinned at Olivia, and they couldn't help but laugh. She combed her fingers through Olivia's long tresses, easing her headache some.

"Do you want to talk about him?" Scarlett asked after a minute or two of silence.

"Not really. It won't change the reality. I'll be alone forever." Olivia dropped back against the bed, staring up at the ceiling as she tried to keep her emotions under control.

Scarlett shifted so she was in Olivia's line of sight. "No, you won't. And your chances with Dawson aren't completely over yet. Just take a few days and go from there."

"Yeah, I think you're right. Besides, I'll be at Ruby's wedding this weekend and then two weeks later is Ella's. What I really need to worry about is what I'm going to do about a job. The kids start school in two weeks. Shaylee said they will head back home next week to get ready for it."

"They're not staying here for Labor Day?" It had always been a fun tradition for the Holts and Justices to go over the top for the weekend around Labor Day, almost a passage into the next year of school. Even though it had been a few years,

Olivia still loved the holiday and tried to make it different from the others.

Olivia made a face and lowered her voice. "No, Shaylee is a little obsessed with the kids excelling in school, so I can imagine she'll want to get them used to their beds at home. I can even see her putting them to bed at six at night."

"What? Really? That's a bit much." Scarlett crossed her eyes, and Olivia burst out laughing, feeling better already.

"Let me play with your hair. That always helps me feel better." She turned Scarlett to face away from her, pulling strands here and there and braiding them together.

Scarlett let her tug and pull for a few minutes before saying, "Why don't you do my hair? Cut it or color it or something. That always makes you feel better."

A shot of excitement whirled up her back, and she said, "Really? You're going to let me play with your gorgeous hair?" She held up a thick shock of the auburn tresses, and Scarlett nodded.

"Yeah, I've been thinking it's time for something different anyway. And if it will help you feel better, let's do it." Scarlett gave her a hug, holding Olivia for several moments before letting go and walking into the shared bathroom down the hall.

Olivia pulled out the hair kit from her suitcase, finding all the tools where they had been when she'd packed several weeks ago. They moved a chair into the bathroom, and Olivia prepped her sister, draping the cape over her and then washing her hair in the sink.

"I don't have any color supplies, or I'd be tempted to try something."

Scarlett smiled. "I've seen some of your coloring clients. You actually do a really good job."

"High praise from a former cynic."

They spent a few minutes talking about styles and

options for how her hair could look and settled on a lob, a long bob that would settle around her shoulders and the front would extend an inch or two longer.

Pulling up sections of the hair and clipping them into place, Olivia's fingers moved on their own, knowing exactly what they needed to do, even after several months of not cutting hair.

"Why don't you open your own salon?" Scarlett said, her eyes closed as she relaxed in the chair.

Olivia paused, not sure what to say about that. "I've never really thought of it. I don't know if I'd be able to figure out all the business setup stuff."

"Oh, please. I could figure that out for you. Or I'm sure a certain CEO could help you spell it out."

When she used her comb to pop Scarlett on the head, her sister flinched and ducked, looking at her through the mirror. "I'm currently in my happy place where I get to beautify you. He's no longer allowed in that happy place."

"Livvy, he told her they were done."

"They looked pretty cozy to me when I walked in there. He told me they'd broken up a few weeks ago, and now she shows up saying she wants to marry him, with his *grandmother's* ring on her finger. He didn't even know what he wanted."

Scarlett bit her lip as she studied Olivia. "You're scared."

"Maybe." She rolled in her bottom lip to keep from crying as she snipped the bottom layer of hair. Pausing, she jabbed her elbow into her side, her hand extended as she looked at Scarlett through the mirror. "What if, hypothetically, we date, and she keeps coming back? I don't think I can take a rollercoaster on one more thing."

Turning in her chair, Scarlett shook her head. "Dawson wouldn't do that. You've known him forever."

"Four years apart can change someone."

"You've spent a good chunk of the last two months

together. Have you noticed anything that signaled he would be that unfeeling?"

Olivia bit the corner of her lip. "No. But everything else has fallen apart in my life. I just assumed my relationships are connected to that kind of luck."

"Okay, let's finish my hair. We'll wait for a final decision on Dawson until you can at least talk to him. Got it?" She looked at Olivia out of the corner of her eye until getting a nod. "And we'll come up with a plan for how to start your own hair business. You could even start with events, like weddings and balls. Or school dances."

Tapping her comb against her mouth lightly, Olivia thought about it. "That's what a normal salon does. But..." She paused as the thought completely formed in her mind. "I remember Love, Austen had a ball, and one of their programs is to do makeovers. What if I ask Meg about those? I could have people come in off the street and then help out when the matchmaking company needs the help."

"That sounds like a great plan. Besides, then you'll get to do what you really love all the time." Scarlett's enthusiasm gave a shot of confidence to Olivia, that her life wasn't over just yet.

Olivia looked at her sister, trying to decide if she was being sarcastic or not. "And what's that?"

"To make people feel beautiful."

Grinning, Olivia leaned over and hugged her sister around the shoulders. "Thank you, Scar. Thank you for everything."

CHAPTER 30

Olivia did her best to focus on the twins over the next week, even though her mind strayed often to the handsome guy way more often than she wanted. Ella had called and texted several times, and Olivia had finally gone over there when her friend said Dawson had gone back to the city.

She'd taken the last ferry back to Boston that Friday, wanting to be early and prepared to help for Ruby's wedding. Ruby had asked her to be the maid of honor right after the show and with Ella's wedding in two weeks, she was destined to be a maid forever, or whatever that old myth was.

Twice a bridesmaid, never a bride. What happens when you're the maid of honor?

The next morning was a flurry of crazy as cameras were set up all over Walden Pond. All the contestants from the show rode together in a limo, getting ready in the trailers onsite. It was fun to catch up with all of them, even if it had only been a little bit of time since they'd all seen each other. If the wedding had been at night, Olivia would have felt déjà vu as everything was set up similarly.

After hair and makeup was taken care of, each of the eleven girls was given a different colored dress. Olivia's was the same pink color as her finale dress, but the cut was different, more relaxed and flowy. She'd have to find Dan and ask him who had designed them. They certainly deserved something for thinking about the woman who had to wear it for several hours.

Once she was ready, she was allowed to walk in and see the bride. "Ruby!"

A look of relief passed over Ruby's face as they embraced. "It's so good to see you again. Are you ready for a few more cameras?"

Grinning, Olivia said, "It's not my wedding they're here for, so I think I'll be fine. Will you?"

Ruby took a few short breaths and said, "I hope so. This is insane. It's been what, six weeks since the show ended? I'm surprised they were able to pull this together that fast."

"I'm not. It will help the next season's viewing if they decide to do another one."

A woman walked into the trailer. "Time for the gown. We've got a schedule to keep, ladies." She moved to the back corner and pulled down a bag, laying it on the small table near where Ruby and Olivia stood.

Pulling out a white dress with a square neckline and a mermaid shape, Ruby's cheeks turned red. "I know it seems different from what I would normally pick, since I don't love attention, but when I put it on, I was like, 'Yes! This is my dress!'" Olivia was surprised at how much Ruby was bouncing, and she knew it was all because she was finally with the love of her life.

Those thoughts made her think of Dawson. The jerk.

Helping Ruby slip the dress on, Olivia did up the individual buttons on the back. "How have you been, Olivia?" her friend asked. "Were you able to find that guy you told me about?"

Again, thoughts of Dawson swarmed her brain. "Yeah. I don't think it will work out after all."

Ruby reached out and touched Olivia's arm, giving her the warm smile Olivia had grown accustomed to on the show. "You never know, girl. Life and love can surprise you in the strangest of ways." The two of them chuckled, knowing that Ruby's relationship with Carson was the epitome of that sentiment.

The door opened again and Dan, the director of *The Suitor*, peeked in. "Showtime, ladies. Everyone else is lined up outside. Someone will bring your bouquet of flowers to you so don't run off trying to find one." He gave them a quick nod and was gone.

The two girls maneuvered out of the trailer in their dresses and heels, and Olivia felt an excitement she'd never felt before as she imagined Carson's face when he saw his bride.

Moving into line, Olivia stood behind Ruby, smoothing out the train. "You look more amazing than a model in a bridal magazine. Carson is going to go crazy."

"I think that's what I'm most excited for." She bit her lip, her eyes scanning the area.

Olivia leaned in to hug the bride and within seconds, she felt someone pull her into line behind Chloe and in front of Ruby. A line of suits stood to the right of the ladies, and Olivia looked up when she saw someone standing next to her. Her mouth went dry, and the world tilted, making her feel dizzy.

"Dawson. What are you doing here?" She took a step back and started to fall, but his strong hands wrapped around her arms, keeping her standing upright.

"I'm the best man." He gave her a shy smile, as if a regular one would crack her into a thousand tiny pieces.

She opened her mouth but couldn't find anything reasonable to say besides, "You didn't say anything about being the best man."

"And you didn't mention being the maid of honor." His lips twitched, and he stared forward. During that time, Olivia couldn't peel her eyes away from him. He looked *good* in a tux, and she wanted to kick her brain for even going there. "I've wanted to talk to you the past few days, I just didn't know how to get you to believe me."

"What? That you hadn't actually broken up with your girlfriend or fiancée or whatever she is to you?" Olivia spat the words in a harsh whisper, and Chloe turned to give her a look. Waving her away, Olivia turned to look at Dawson.

"Ex-girlfriend." He enunciated the words in her ear, and the sound of it hummed throughout her entire body. Darn traitorous nervous system!

"What about all the announcements she made on social media and the news?" Olivia needed to know for sure, and it felt great to get a little of the frustration out.

Before he could answer, someone came down the line and shushed them, directing them to catch up to Chloe and the guy who stood with her.

Looping her arm through his, Olivia wished she didn't feel like she was touching an electrical socket. It made her want to lean into him, to kiss his lips again and erase everything that had come between them in the past two weeks.

The procession was faster than Olivia had expected, and she let go of Dawson's arm to move to the bride's side, glancing up at the pine trees. The smell of the woods reminded her of their time at the cabin, and it was still amazing to think that three months ago, she'd met most of these people.

She looked over at Dawson from time to time, and he seemed to be trained on her, making heat race all the way to the tips of her ears. After the vows had been read, the couple kissed and took off down the aisle. As she joined up with Dawson to lead the pairs after the bride and groom, she was grateful they'd chosen not to have a reception. There was no way she could survive a night where she would have to dance with the attractive man to her left.

CHAPTER 31

The luncheon took place shortly after the ceremony. Olivia and Dawson had been directed to the main table, sitting on one side of the newlyweds. They'd made it through the best man and maid-of-honor speeches, and the crowd was mingling, congratulating the lovebirds and enjoying the dessert table.

After trying one of the desserts Olivia couldn't pronounce, she was blown away by the flavor. Taking an extra piece, she moved back to the table, needing to take off the heels for a few minutes. She wasn't sure how women could wear them like athletic shoes, running in them in action movies. She was just lucky she didn't break an ankle when she wore them.

In that thought process, it took her a moment to realize someone had come to sit by her. At first, she thought it was Dawson, and she wanted to ignore him. When a light tap touched her shoulder, she turned to see Meg grinning at her.

"Enjoying the desserts? They're some of my favorites too. Lexi, Brennen's girlfriend, makes them. I hire her as often as I can because she always does a fantastic job."

"Yes, this is my new favorite pastry." Wiping at the corners of her mouth with a napkin, Olivia asked, "How are you, Meg?"

The blonde smiled, and it brightened every part of her face. "I'm fabulous, but I'm here to talk about you, and not me."

Olivia froze, not sure where this conversation was going. "Okay…"

"I have a source that says you're an amazing hairdresser. I have had plans for our makeover clients for months now but have never been able to find the right fit. So, what I'm wondering is if you'd be interested in heading up that department?"

Letting out a gasp, Olivia felt her heart pounding in her chest. "You want me to run your makeovers?"

Meg nodded. "We have some options on space as well. I originally designed my third floor as the 'makeover room,' but the tenant next door is moving out soon. It would be perfect for a salon, and while the makeovers wouldn't be enough to keep you in business, having a storefront on Beacon Street would help get clients."

"So, you're saying that I can start my own business, but I would already have a few clients through the makeover program to get me started?" When Meg confirmed it, Olivia threw her arms around the matchmaker, tears pricking at the corners of her eyes. "Thank you," she whispered before sitting back.

"No, thank you. I've seen a lot from you, Olivia. On the show, and from all the referrals recommending you for this position, I would say you've got some great friends. Come in and talk to me about it when you get a chance. I know you've got another wedding coming up soon, so maybe after that's all over?"

"That would be perfect."

Meg turned to move away before turning back. "Oh, I was going to give you this envelope. It's a mystery but don't open it until you get back to Nantucket. It will all explain itself." She winked at Olivia before joining her fiancé at one of the other tables.

The package was a large manila envelope that had been taped several times. She recognized the writing as Meg's, which confused her even more. What could be inside that they hadn't already talked about?

She shook the package as though it were a Christmas present, and she'd know exactly what was in it from the thump or jingle that followed. Nothing.

Ruby walked up to the table and gave her a hug. "I'm married!" she squealed softly. Olivia felt the excitement and nodded.

"You two are going to be amazing. I can't wait to see what you do together."

"We're off. Thank you a million times for being here today. It meant a lot, especially since…" Ruby looked toward the table, and she knew the void of her parents' absence still hurt.

"I wouldn't have missed it. Have a great honeymoon, and I'll see you when you get back."

They hugged again, and Ruby said, "I wish you all the luck in the world. I hope you have news of your own when our honeymoon is over."

Olivia gave her a strange look before letting her go, as Carson stood behind waiting. The couple left in a white limo, and Olivia sighed. The fairytale continued for those two.

But they didn't go without bumps in the road.

"I'm heading out. Do you need a ride somewhere?" Dawson leaned one hand on the table as he looked down at her.

Shaking her head, she said, "I think I'll help clean up here.

I haven't talked to some of the girls yet. But, thank you, Dawson. I appreciate the offer." She gave him a genuine smile, wanting to somehow get back the friendship they'd shared over a lifetime. To do that, she'd have to swallow some of her pride.

His face showed a glimmer of disappointment before replacing it with a simple mask of a smile. He glanced at the envelope on the table and pointed to it. "What's that?"

Olivia shrugged. "I'm not sure. Something Meg gave me to open when I head back to Nantucket."

He nodded, stuffing his hands into his pants pockets. "That's cool. Okay, well, I'll see you soon then."

She wished she could berate herself for watching him walk away, his movements agile and quick. He looked good on an average day but for some reason, the tux just made her all giggly inside. Maybe it was because it represented a wedding, and as much as she knew he was out of her reach, she still longed for it.

Standing, she went to mingle with some of the other girls from the show, lighter than she had been in a while. With a job opportunity as well as the chance to be self-employed, there was hope to keep her family afloat. At least it was something to look forward to.

CHAPTER 32

After visiting her mother Sunday morning, Olivia took the ferry back to Nantucket. In all the years her family had owned a house there, she'd never left as much as she had that summer. Not much had changed with her mother's condition but with a renewed hope that they weren't going to have to cut off all care for her once the life insurance money ran out, it was more peaceful this time.

Ella was waiting for her when the boat docked. It seemed like she hadn't had anyone to talk to in days; there were several minutes where Olivia wondered if she'd even taken a breath.

"How was the wedding? Dawson said it was a nice, simple affair."

Dawson. As much as she'd tried to push away thoughts of him since she'd seen him the day before, it seemed as though those thoughts multiplied, occupying more of her brain than anything else.

"It was a lovely wedding. Small and intimate if you don't count the dozens of cameras set up all around." The two of them laughed at that as Ella pulled the SUV out of the parking lot. Olivia had packed light for the quick trip, and the duffel bag was in the backseat, along with her purse. She'd placed the manila envelope on her lap and had forgotten about it until Ella pointed to it.

"What's that?"

Looking down, Olivia picked it up. "I'm not sure yet. Meg just said to wait and open it when I got to Nantucket."

"Well, you're here now. Open it!"

Olivia rolled in both lips, feeling the nerves take over. She'd survived over twenty-four hours with the thing in her possession, why was she so worried about it now?

Pulling back some of the tape, she opened the corner and slid her finger inside, breaking through the top of it. Dumping the contents out on her lap, she frowned. A bunch of odd-shaped packages sat there.

Picking up the first one, she read aloud, "'Number three. Find this in something you would take your clothes in on a trip.' Why would Meg give me a scavenger hunt?" Or could it be from Dawson? She mentally brushed that off, remembering the look of surprise and indifference on his face when he saw the envelope at the wedding. As romantic as it would be if he'd done it, hopes and reality were two different things.

Ella made a face and shrugged her shoulders. "What does the first one say?"

Searching through the five packages, she finally found the first one. "Open at the dock." Ella put on the brakes and pulled over to the side of the road.

Olivia eyes her. "What did you do that for?"

"Because we don't want to be too far from the dock. What if we have to do something there?" She clapped her hands together, a smile beaming at Olivia.

Pointing to all the packages in her lap, Olivia laughed. "I don't think we'll have to really be there but let me open it and see." The package was small, and she wondered what would go with the docks and something that small. A fishhook?

Out of the package she pulled two charms, one was a pair of scissors and the other was a vintage mirror. "They're beautiful."

"And they will go perfectly on your charm bracelet. You'd better get those on there before they fall between the seats. I think one of my favorite earrings is still down there somewhere."

Olivia nodded, working the charms onto the bracelet. She held up the bracelet ring and shook her arm a little, loving the sound of the little objects.

"Where do you have to go for number two? We should probably move before we block all traffic on this road."

Locating the second package, Olivia said, "Open in a car." She laughed, and Ella pulled back onto the road, looking over every few seconds to see what was inside the much bigger package.

Opening the long rectangular package, Olivia found several pamphlets on different travel spots throughout the States.

Ella turned her nose up. "What's that supposed to represent?"

"The only thing I can think is that I've always wanted to go on a road trip across the U.S. These are a bunch of things I could see on a road trip."

"Did I know you wanted to do that? Cause I can't remember that."

Olivia didn't know either. She'd told a few people over the past few months, but she couldn't remember them all.

Clapping her hands together, Ella bounced in the driver's seat. "Open number three! This is exciting!"

"Open near the airport." The airport? What could possibly be a gift connected to the airport?

Ella wove in and out of pedestrians and cars, speeding to get to the small island airport. As they pulled off the side of the road, Olivia could feel adrenaline pouring through her, the excitement growing with each small gift. How would Meg have known about all this?

Slipping her finger behind the flap, she opened the envelope and pulled out tickets for a flight. She searched the destination and saw Paris. "Tickets to Paris!"

"What?" Ella's reaction made Olivia giggle and when she showed them to her friend, Ella went crazy. "You can come visit me! Oh, whoever is doing this is seriously the best gift giver ever. I need this person to be in charge of me for Christmas." She winked at Olivia, and something about it made Olivia suspicious.

"What are you hiding? Do you know who this is from?" She narrowed her eyes, trying to see any sign of lying.

Ella held up her hands, her wide eyes showing her innocence. "I don't know anything. I just picked you up at that dock, remember?" Olivia stared at her for a few more seconds, finally deciding she was telling the truth.

"Can we move onto number four?" Ella asked with a grin.

"Maybe we should stop opening them. How can you top a trip to Paris?" Olivia tried to keep a straight face and was rewarded with a look of horror from Ella.

"Are you kidding? You can't stop now. I have to know what's bigger than Paris."

With two packages left, it wasn't hard to find number four. This time, the writing was much smaller, and the instructions were numbered.

"Take packages 4 and 5 to Brant Point Lighthouse. Go on the walkway all the way to the lighthouse. Once there, only open package number 4."

Ella found a spot to turn around and whipped back in the direction of the harbor. "Too bad they didn't start with this one first. It looks like it might be near dark soon. Hopefully, you can see what you need to."

Once they pulled up to the end of the paved road, Ella motioned for her to get out. "I'll just wait here. I don't want anyone to tow our only mode of transportation here."

Olivia slid out of the SUV with a package in each hand. Her heart beat faster with each step, pounding against her ribcage as the suspense built. What would be so important to go through such an elaborate ruse? With each footstep, she thought about who the gifts could have been from. Was it just an extra gift from the people at *The Suitor*? Maybe they'd forgotten about it and wanted to do something fun to present them to her.

Shaking her head, she knew that was ridiculous. The Bourdens? They'd been appreciative of all she'd done with the kids in the past two months. But the gifts so far had been more intimate, and Olivia hadn't shared such details with her employer. Again, her mind drifted to Dawson, the deep-brown eyes focused on her face, the corners of his mouth turned up in a soft expression. As much as she'd tried to fight it, heart break was just around the corner.

The sun had almost set, the last few rays of sun just barely lighting up the night sky. She glanced down the path, lights flickering at the end of the boardwalk. She picked up the pace and reached a hand to her mouth in shock as she saw flower petals all over, along with several candles set out on the boardwalk and the railing.

She set the fifth package on the railing and opened package number four. Inside it was another package with more instructions. This time, it was flat, as if it contained papers. Would someone be gifting her this lighthouse? It was beautiful, and she loved to come here but what use did she have for a lighthouse?

Slow down, mind. Just read the instructions.

The paper on the package was lengthier than the others, and she leaned up against the rail to read it.

"When you went on *The Suitor*, you started a journey that wasn't finished with the last taping. Love, Austen guarantees a match of several men, in your case, but three are pulled that are considered the 'best match,' meaning the two of you match in more than one category. While your picture showed up in the envelope as a good match for Carson Carver, your match score with him was a 75%. Inside the envelope are the three men you match with at over a 90% match rate, the first two being 92% and the last one 97%. There have been a lot of things you've given up in your life, Olivia, but love shouldn't be one of them."

Seeing no other instructions on the front or back, she carefully opened the envelope, her stomach in her throat. She pulled out some pictures, looking at the first one and then the second, both good-looking guys. She paused a moment before pulling out the third picture, knowing it was the best match for her.

Closing her eyes, she pulled it from below the other two and slowly opened her eyes. There was the picture of the milk-chocolate eyes she'd fallen in love with, the smile that made her go weak in the knees. She sank to the boards and stared at the picture of Dawson.

Tears flowed freely, and she wished he'd been there. She needed to apologize for being so harsh at the wedding. But she wasn't sure how she matched up to someone who was already taken.

A sound on the boardwalk startled her, and she looked up to see Dawson taking a few strides toward her from the direction of the lighthouse. He leaned down and lifted her chin, a hesitant smile on his face.

"You did all this?" she asked, sniffling.

Reaching into his pocket, he pulled out a tissue and handed it to her. "I thought we might need these tonight." He turned his head and asked, "Are you okay that I'm here?"

"Are you engaged?"

A smile played at his lips. "At the moment, no. Liv, I'm not with Adelyn, and I don't want to be. We had some good times, but I've never felt for her the way I do for you."

It took several seconds for Olivia to process the meaning there. Her breath caught at his last words, but her mind wasn't so easily convinced. "Did you know about the match thing?"

"Parker mentioned it to me a few days before Carson and Ruby's wedding. Meg had been trying to get me to schedule an appointment to go over the matches, and I kept forgetting, conveniently." He reached forward and wrapped his arms around her.

"I wanted it to be you. I think once I started reading about the match results on this envelope," she held it up to show him, her insides aflutter. "I hoped you'd be in there."

He pulled back, and his grin went from ear to ear. "I'm glad to hear that. Because I want you to know, that when I told you I'd broken up with Adelyn, I considered us through. She pretended to be engaged on her own, and I didn't do anything to encourage it."

Olivia nodded. "I know that now. I was just worried that it was all for real. When I saw the two of you in the kitchen, I—"

"I promise, that was all her. I tried to look all over the house for you after you dashed out of there. And then I came to the Bourdens."

Olivia nodded. "I know. I heard you talking to Shaylee."

"You should open package five," he said, his expression nervous. Olivia looked down and saw that his hand was shaking.

She reached up and pulled the small square package off the railing, sitting back down. Instead of trying to be careful this time, she ripped the paper free when she saw no instructions. The gift was a beautiful red jewelry box. Dawson reached forward and gently took it from her, moving so he was on one knee. He flipped open the box to reveal the beautiful antique ring.

"This was my mother's ring." He gave her a small smile.

"What happened to your grandmother's?" Olivia asked. She remembered seeing it on Adelyn's finger when she'd come to the pool party and a sense of relief washed over her that Dawson hadn't presented it to her. With all the excitement evolving around this moment, she knew that down the road, it would be hard to look at it and not think of the other girl.

"I gave it to Jeremy," he said with a smile. A few seconds passed, and his face sobered as he let out a deep breath. "Olivia Elinor Justice, will you be my best friend for life and marry me?"

Throwing her arms around his neck, she whispered, "Yes!" in his ear. He pulled back enough for his lips to meet hers, soft at first. He deepened the kiss, and Olivia felt it all the way to her toes. When they broke apart, he rested his forehead on hers, staring into her eyes and grinning.

"I love you, Liv. I think I've always loved you, ever since we were kids."

Olivia laughed. "Me too." She leaned forward and gave him a peck on the lips before saying, "I love you, Dawson. Thanks for proving dreams do come true."

EPILOGUE

*E*lla and Tony got married on a beautiful day the Saturday before Labor Day and left on their honeymoon to Jamaica after the reception. Dawson and Olivia left Nantucket, and she worked on her future business next to Love, Austen, something Olivia still couldn't stop smiling about.

The day she'd brought Dawson to visit her mother had been a good day, and Peggy had even recognized him, getting excited for the wedding and talking about old times. By the end of the visit, she'd slipped into a coma and died just a few days later. The happiness and excitement on her face made it all worth it to Olivia, that last glimpse of her mother ingrained into her memory now.

Jeremy proposed to Scarlett soon after, and Olivia couldn't have been happier for the two of them. With his calm personality, he balanced Scarlett out better than anyone she'd known.

The second week of October, Dawson and Olivia set out on a three-week road trip across the country, stopping at several of tourist attractions along the way. When they'd made it to Oregon, they stopped at an information booth, and Dawson pulled out a pamphlet that talked about eloping near Crater Lake.

They walked outside, and he said, "Have you decided on a day or a place you want to get married?"

Olivia blew out a breath, feeling bad she hadn't come to a decision on either. "I don't want the wedding to be big. I loved the simplicity of both Ruby and Ella's weddings. I just don't know if I want to wait that long for the wedding and all the planning..." She let her voice trail off.

"What if we get married tomorrow? We could spend the last few days of the trip on our honeymoon and then head back home." He handed her the pamphlet, the corners of his lips turning up.

Reading through the leaflet, Olivia looked up at him. "This looks amazing. I want to say let's go for it, but there are a few people who would kill us."

"My sister being one of them." Dawson laughed. "I know Scarlett had been pushing to have a double wedding, but this is about us."

Taking in a deep breath, she said, "Let's do it."

The next several hours were spent getting all the paper-work signed and finding something suitable for the two of them to wear. The biggest hang-up was finding someone to marry them. Instead of the next day, the ceremony was scheduled for two o'clock two days from then.

Olivia stood on a plateau just below where the ceremony would take place. She'd done her makeup and curled her hair in loose waves; the simple white lace dress touched the ground, making it so she had to hold it up when she walked. The photographer they'd hired brought a simple bouquet and worked to make sure everything was right.

"Are you ready to go?" a familiar voice said behind her.

Whirling around, Olivia let out a cry, doing all she could to not burst into tears.

"Ella, what are you doing here?" Movement behind her brought Scarlett into view. "Scar? How did you know to come?"

The two of them grinned, and Ella said, "Dawson called. I hopped on the first flight out of Paris and just arrived here about two hours ago."

"He didn't want you to regret getting married without all of us here." Scarlett pulled her in for a hug. "He even offered for it to be a double elopement, if you didn't mind."

Olivia was sure her heart would burst. "I would love that. Are you okay getting married here?"

Scarlett looked around and nodded, eyes wide. "Have you seen the view up there? It's amazing."

The photographer brought another bouquet of flowers, holding them until Scarlett took off her sweater, revealing a simple white blouse with small rosettes dispersed around it. Her white tulle skirt puffed out to the side and with her hair already twisted, she looked like an effortless bride.

Olivia reached forward and squeezed her sister's hand. "I can't believe you're here, and that we're getting married."

"This is way better than planning a full wedding."

Ella sighed. "Why didn't I do this? At least I'm here to give you both away."

"We're ready up top, if you ladies are." The woman smiled at them before snapping a few pictures.

"I'm ready if you are," Olivia said, looking at Scarlett.

Her sister nodded. "Let's do this."

Ella took her place between the two of them, holding out her arms, and the three of them walked to the lookout.

Scarlett had been right about the beauty of the lake. The bright blue next to the trees and steep incline made her tear up at such a view.

Feeling a hand wrap around her waist, she felt Dawson's lips close to her ear. "You're the most beautiful bride I've ever seen."

Twisting in his arms, she looked into his brown eyes and couldn't help but smile. She was about to kiss him when a man cleared his throat next to them.

"Are you ready to start the vows?" the justice of the peace asked.

Dawson and Olivia nodded, as did Jeremy and Scarlett.

The vows took only a few minutes, but Olivia kept thinking about being Mrs. Dawson Holt, breathing a sigh of relief when the man finally said, "I now pronounce you husbands and wives. You may now kiss the brides."

Olivia bit her bottom lip, not quite believing she was now married to her long-time crush. Dawson leaned forward and kissed her softly, before moving to pick her up. She wrapped her arms around his neck and pulled him close. She'd almost forgotten they weren't alone when the man said, "We'll be over here. We just need you to sign the documents, and you'll be good to go."

Stealing another kiss before Dawson set her down, she whispered, "It's official. The man of my dreams is now my husband."

Dawson laughed. "And the girl next door is now my wife. Here's to a life of fulfilled dreams." He kissed her longer this time, and by the time he pulled away, she had to breathe deep to fill her lungs. Who would've thought that after all they'd been through together, they'd get to do life as man and wife?

"What's next for us, Mrs. Holt?" Dawson asked, his face beaming. He set her down as they walked over to sign the papers.

Interlacing her fingers with his, Olivia felt the same electricity she'd felt time and time again. "I'm not sure yet, but whatever it is, I want to do it with you."

* * *

Continue Abby and Greyson's story in *Austen, Edited!*

* * *

Thank you for reading *Matched, Austen!* If you enjoyed it, I would love to see a review from you. You can also subscribe to Britney's newsletter here:
Subscribe to Britney's List
Or join her Facebook Reader Group

ALSO BY BRITNEY M. MILLS

The Love, Austen Series

Love, Austen

Austen, Party of Two

Austen Unscripted

Matched, Austen

Austen, Edited

The International Billionaire Series

The Australian Billionaire

The French Billionaire

The British Billionaire

The Vegas Billionaire

The Italian Billionaire

Rosemont High Baseball Series

The Perfect Play

The Perfect Game

The Perfect Catch

The Perfect Steal

The Perfect Hit

Christmas at Coldwater Creek Series

Love in a Blizzard

Love in the Lights

Love in a Snapshot

Love in the Details

Sage Creek Small Town Series

Loving His Flower Girl

Loving His Reporter Girl

Join Britney's newsletter

Get the latest updates on new releases and other fun tidbits!

www.ingramcontent.com/pod-product-compliance
Lightning Source LLC
Chambersburg PA
CBHW021333190726
48288CB00003B/1094